Roughly Thrown Dice

Roughly Thrown Dice

By Steve Borst

CITIOFBOOKS, INC.
3736 Eubank NE Suite A1
Albuquerque, NM 87111-3579
www.citiofbooks.com

Hotline: 1 (877) 389-2759
Fax: 1 (505) 930-7244

Ordering Information:
Quantity sales. Special discounts are available on quantity purchases by corporations, associations, and others. For details, contact the publisher at the address above.

Printed in the United States of America.

ISBN-13:   Softcover   979-8-89391-866-3
             eBook   979-8-89391-867-0

Library of Congress Control Number: 2025917212

Table of Contents

A Night at The Tubes 7
How the Captors Came and Swept the Scene 11
What the Morning Brought 15
How the Captives Were Met 19
Cast of Characters. 27
How the Captives Passed the Time 29
A Short Book of Dreams 35
A Second Day of Dreams 45
How the Government Set to Work 51
The Sergeant-at-Arms' Tale 55
The Executive's Tale 63
What the Physiologist Heard. 71
The Heiress's Tale 75
The Physiologist's Tale. 81
Where Did the Ski Bum Go?. 89
Operation Haystack 93
Old Fitzgerald. 97
Clay and Sandy 109
The Event Planner's Tale 113
The Release of the Heiress. 117
The Musician's Tale. 121
The Physician's Tale. 131
The Death of the Physician. 141
The First Engineer's Tale 143
Green Thomas 147
The Ski Bum and the Gentleman 153
The Physiologist's Second Tale. 155
The Bartender's Tale 159
Higher and Sunnier. 165

The Lawyer's Tale 167
Click to Enlarge 171
Operation Lily Pad 179
The Death of the Navy Pilot 181
The Raid 185
Postscript 189

A Night at The Tubes

On a clear night, driving toward Mount Lasser on route 324, coming in from the flatlands, you can see The Tubes from fifty miles away. Its pair of beacons, set forty-five degrees apart, are like an overhead tractor beam pulling you in, an irresistible force. Set halfway up the mountainside, The Tubes is a restaurant and après ski disco that attracts a high-end crowd. The overall design resembles nothing so much as a pair of toilet paper rolls, each with one end cut at an angle and the two beveled faces joined. The design of The Tubes actually began with rolls of toilet paper. Set on a steeply sloping promontory of exposed rock halfway up Mount Lasser and above the other buildings of the ski resort, The Tubes is propped up high on concrete pillars, cast over steel beams, which are joined solidly to the bedrock. The open end of each tube is entirely glass and light shines out from each end far over the valley below. A kitchen and service building connects the tubes and on its roof, is a helipad affording VIP access for private parties for high-rollers.

The architect, Roland White, was a college student at the time he designed The Tubes and suite mate of the Physiologist Evet St. Rob, whom you will meet in the next pages. There had been a national contest among prominent architects to design an exclusive nightclub for this difficult, solid-rock and uneven site. One of the entrants was a professor of White's and he set up a mock competition for his students. While other students spent months laboring over their designs and models, White, who was regarded by both his teachers and peers as a brilliant procrastinator, tackled the project only at the last moment and intended to solve it with a single all-nighter.

The Chaumont Arms, where he lived, was an apartment building converted to a dorm and White had his work desk set up in the living room of the suite. The four suite mates had painted that living room in the style of Jackson Pollock. After moving out the furniture and covering the floor, they had flung paint of every color at the white walls, using brushes, turkey basters and whatever else was on hand.

With his design due the next day, White began the evening by getting drunk. When he set to work, he began with several balsa wood and cardboard models, as he preferred this method to drawing. After a few hours, he was growing frustrated and by midnight, he was in a rage, cursing and blaming inanimate objects around him, steel rules and Exacto knives, over the protests of his roommates who were trying to sleep. At one point, White took his latest balsa wood model into the bathroom, set it in the bathtub and after dousing it with lighter fluid, set fire to it. The bathroom had been decorated in appalling taste by the Physiologist, who had covered the faucets, towel bars, medicine cabinet, exposed steam pipes and even the toilet with metallic contact paper covered in Day-Glo paisley and psychedelic designs. In the morning, White was found asleep at his desk. In front of him sat the model, consisting of the two tubes joined at an acute angle and set onto the promontory of red clay using slender sticks of balsa wood. Beside the model sat a drained bottle of Jägermeister. Discarded toilet paper littered the floor. That afternoon at the jury, Roland White's design created a sensation among his professors. It so happened that the national competition, the actual competition, was stalled. The directors of the Mount Lasser Resort were not happy with any of the designs they had seen. At this point, White's professor had an idea. The two worked together to produce a set of drawings and a more professional model of White's design, which was submitted, and to everyone's surprise, eventually accepted. By then, White himself had become disgruntled in a vague sort of way and had checked out of the university, which he liked to refer to as a 'glorified anus'. He disappeared for good into the hinterlands. None-the-less, the design is still credited to him. Whether he ever pursued a career in architecture is unknown, at least to me.

The northwest face of Mount Lasser is clearly defined plane, like that of the Matterhorn, but not nearly as steep. That side has the best slopes and the most snow. However, it was a near-record season for snow and it was a problem keeping the road into the resort clear. Those who drove in negotiated a dark gauntlet between high walls of plowed snow.

The other choice was to park below and take a tram to the lodge. The upper mountain was a bit top-heavy. There was a lot of snow up there, too much snow, but the management was keeping a close eye on it and, so far, it seemed to be holding together well. It goes without saying that closing the resort, even temporarily, would have resulted in a big loss of revenue.

The evening of January 27 was a typical in-season Friday at the Mount Lasser Resort. The hotel and the slopes were full of skiers. By six, the sun was setting and the lights had begun to come on for night skiing. The bar and disco at The Tubes were beginning to fill up. Nothing yet suggested the events that were to follow and which we all remember. The Chameleons, led by Ian Underwood, were playing The Tubes that night. They were fresh off appearances at such trendy venues as Dionysos in Miami and the Goth Hotel in Kentucky and they were beginning to garner a national reputation. Their music was selling and they were beginning to get beyond their initial reputation as a cover band. It was true - they didn't write many songs; they just did new arrangements that were significantly different, and in many cases better than the original. Louis Armstrong wasn't a 'cover' act. He was a great writer who specialized in new arrangements of existing songs. Same for Paul Butterfield. The Chameleons did and still do hard rock, art rock, the blues, and country, hence the name. They even do a couple of flamenco numbers, one an original and one that was first recorded by Manitas de Plata and Jose Reyes.

As the Chameleons took the stage, there was a mixed group on and around the dance floor, among them bikers, business and preppy types, a TV news crew, and a reunion of Black fraternity brothers. The Tubes had a high-end clientele and was not a watering hole for locals, due to its remote location, hundred-dollar cover charge and twenty dollar drinks. Between the bar and dance floor, a spectacular floor-to-ceiling aquarium served as a partial room divider. Patrons could see their companions' faces through the water and also appreciate a colorful display of tropical fish.

By the end of the first set, there were maybe a hundred people on the dance floor; some drinking, some dancing. The effects of alcohol were setting in and there was beginning to be some mixing between groups.

There was a light show above the dance floor. One pair of dancers stood out and received a spotlight from the crew: a white-haired biker in full leathers and a beautiful dark-haired woman, who is a well-known TV news reporter. She was dressed in a sharkskin pants-suit with a black-magenta iridescent sheen. He was not tall, but was powerfully built. She was several inches taller. The two stepped into the spotlight and all eyes were immediately upon them as they became lost to each other in the bands of primal color that swept over them. The Chameleons challenged the two dancers by switching abruptly from a blues number to the cha-cha. The couple switched to the cha-cha without missing a beat and for that they received a hand from onlookers.

How the Captors Came
and Swept the Scene

At around one thirty PM, while the band was on its second break, the guests heard what they thought was muffled thunder high on the mountain above and a few may have thought that strange, as it was a clear night full of stars. What they had heard were actually charges of TNT set off high above them on the mountain. Next was heard a crack as sharp as a billiards break and following that, a rumbling that grew to a roaring and tearing until eventually it sounded like a thousand trains surrounding them on all sides, above and below. Then everyone knew what had happened. The house lights came on. The party was over. The alcohol had drained right out of them, leaving each of them stone cold sober. A veil had been lifted from their eyes and the harshness of the new reality was just beginning to be apparent. The revelers ran to the few windows, hoping to get a view of the mountainside above. But above the surface of the snow lay such a thick blanket of snow mist that they could see nothing of the havoc outside.

A rolling and heaving river of snow had passed right under them, passed under The Tubes. The building was jolted and shaken while the guests themselves stood frozen, paralyzed under the bright lights. The building was sorely tested but the supporting pillars proved strong enough and it did not fail. As the avalanche continued past them, moving further down into the valley, slowly, the roaring began to subside until at last, the room was deadly silent. The guests looked around at one another and no one among them spoke a single word. After ten minutes of agonizing silence, the guests heard the thick whir of helicopter blades overhead. On the roof of the central building, the one joining the two tubes, was a helicopter pad, one that was sometimes used for VIP events. In the 80s, the Rolling Stones had thrown a party for about two hundred guests at The Tubes and the Stones themselves had arrived by helicopter. Over the years, many celebrities had been flown into The Tubes.

There was a lot of noise on the roof and then suddenly the power to the building was lost and every light in The Tubes went out. The snow mist had come in through broken windows and filled the air around the revelers. It was so dark on the dance floor and at the bar that people could not make out the face even of someone who was standing right next to them. Soon after, six assailants brandishing assault rifles, stormed the dance floor by way of a hallway beside the kitchen. An overhead spray of bullets brought down a rain of noise and glass fragments from windows and light fixtures. More cold fog rushed in through the broken windows. Several bullets struck the aquarium and because of the type of glass it was made of, the bullets did not shatter the whole sheet of glass the way they had shattered the windows. Instead, bullet holes were left, from which small spouts of water emanated that would continue to flow long after there was no living person left in The Tubes.

The revelers stood shivering, as none of them were dressed for the cold. A cloud of snow mist lay thick between them and they could see little except the beams of flashlights sweeping across the room.

Then all the flashlights were trained on one man, who spoke to them in perfect English with a French accent. "When I choose you, one of us will lead you down that hallway and up the stairs to the helicopter. Any sign of hesitation on your part and we will not hesitate to *kill* you. I hope that is clear to everyone in this room. Your lives depend on it." With that, there was another overhead spray of machine gun fire and then with great speed and deliberation, each of the guests was questioned by this same man. Some were chosen, some were passed over. His aim, it would later be learned, was to choose those with money, those who could be ransomed, and as a result, he chose a somewhat older group. The assailants took the cell phones of all and used thermite to destroy them in several metal trash cans. One man made a break down the stairwell. They chased him down, shot and killed him. Of course, if he had made it to the ground floor, he could never have made it to the outside because of an impenetrable barrier of snow. One by one, the hostages were led up the stairs to the roof, where a troop transport helicopter hovered precariously on a pad that was too small for it.

The helicopter was over-loaded with nineteen captives and six terrorists. The seats had been stripped out in advance and the hostages were crammed together on the floor of the cargo bay. From the rooftop of The Tubes, the overstuffed bird lurched forward. It would be a cold, dark, windy and noisy trip and the hostages could be glad they were forced together, as this conserved their body heat. Almost right away, trouble started between two of the hostages. Over the roar of the helicopter blades, one Martin Pelli, a business executive, proclaimed to the heavens, the indignity of his position.

"I don't know who you are or who you think you are, but you will pay a price for this. I am an American citizen, an important person and not someone to trifle with."

"Shut up, you spoiled brat" called out the biker from the dance floor. "We're all in this together."

The captives were packed close together lying on the floor of the cargo bay. Pelli was pressed close against a woman. His head was right behind hers and she was looking away from him. He looked over her black and shining hair. There was just a little light coming from the cockpit and it lit the curve of her cheek. Martin Pelli was still a little drunk and he felt like he was looking at the full moon shining. The woman was beautiful, but she had acne scars across her cheek and the faint purple shadows in the depressions neatly made the craters of the moon for Martin. He felt a protective urge toward her and he moved in close and put his cheek against hers. Delores del Rio turned and punched him in the gut. "Asshole! Keep your hands to yourself."

For the most part, the captives were quiet as they hurtled through the night on their way toward a destination they could not imagine.

What the Morning Brought

The avalanche buried all of the night skiers and also those who were walking the grounds. It also buried the only road into the resort. The hotel was damaged and there were some casualties inside. It was several hours before the rescue effort would begin. Morning light would reveal the full measure of the devastation that had occurred.

The Mount Lasser Hotel was not in the direct path of the avalanche, but somewhat off to the side. It was buried in snow up to its second story windows and those who were trapped inside were relatively safe. They used their cell phones to get out first word of the attack, as did two members of the ski patrol, who had been above the avalanche at the time. In the first couple of hours, those two from the ski patrol removed six skiers from the snow, three of whom were already dead. In the early hours of the morning, they were joined by fully equipped rescue teams who arrived by snowmobile. By daylight, rescuers with dogs were combing the mountainside. A full-scale rescue operation was underway. The media were also on the scene and images of devastation were being broadcast around the world. In total, the rescuers would pull one hundred and ten night-skiers and others from the snow. People don't last long when buried deep in snow, what with the impact, cold and lack of oxygen. Almost all were dead.

All morning, Medevac helicopters from two local hospitals ferried the victims down the mountainside. There were so many victims that there was not time to fly them directly to the hospital. Instead they were brought to a parking lot at the base of the mountain and were taken the rest of the way by ambulances and other rescue vehicles. There were only ten survivors for the short term and five of them would die in hospital over the next days.

It would take more time to rescue all the remaining guests at the disco. They had priority because there was no power, and thus no heat, in the building. Many others were trapped in the hotel. Some waited a day for the road to be cleared and others were given snowshoes and were able to escape out of second-story windows from which they made the trek of nearly a mile to open roadway, some dragging their luggage.

As evacuation neared completion, authority began to switch from rescue and medical units to the police and finally to the FBI, upon their arrival. As the accounting of the living and the dead progressed on site, the FBI were able, by process of elimination and through interviews with survivors, to begin assembling a list of the hostages.

That afternoon, there was a White House announcement and press conference in the Brady Press Room. President McKelly stepped up to the bank of microphones.

"Good morning, my fellow Americans. I am sad to report that our great nation has come under a deadly terror attack. Late last night, terrorists assaulted the Mount Lasser Ski Resort in California. They caused an avalanche that killed at least ninety-five people and they have taken between twenty and thirty Americans to an unknown location where, presumably, they are being held as hostages. Today our thoughts and prayers are with the victims of this horrific crime and with their families. We have very little information at this time and so my message will be brief. We do not yet know the identity of the assailants, other than that they are presumed to be foreign nationals. Nor do we know anything about their motivation. As events develop, we will keep the American people informed. And I promise you this. The attack we have experienced is no doubt designed to intimidate the American people and to undermine our morale. Let the cowards who perpetrated this outrageous act know that we are a strong people and that this evil deed will not go unpunished. The full resources of the federal government will be employed to bring these criminals to justice and to aid the victims and their families. The Press Secretary will now take your brief questions."

The Secretary moved up to the mic. "Jim?"

"Do we know if all those buried on the ski slopes have been recovered?"

"Full recovery of individuals buried in the snow will take another

24 hours. Bear in mind that with each passing hour, the chances of being recovered alive are diminished. Carol?"

"Do we know how the hostages were removed?"

"They were removed from The Tubes restaurant and nightclub by helicopter. The building has a helipad on the roof. I can't tell you any more than that. Chicago Times, I'm sorry I don't know your name."

"Jay Klein. Do we know who the hostages are and specifically if they are wealthy individuals who might be able to pay ransom?"

"We are working on that list right now but cannot yet release it because it is not complete and for other reasons as well. Paying ransom to terrorists is against the law. Bill?"

"Is there any chance that this is a case of domestic terror?"

"We don't think so at this time. That's all the questions we have time for right now."

While the President was making his announcement, nineteen captives together with their six captors were packed into a military jet hurtling high over the Pacific. The rear seats of the aircraft had been stripped out to accommodate a greater number of passengers, who were all packed into the cargo bay. They would have been glad for the close quarters, as the interior of the plane was freezing. They had some loose blankets and sleeping bags with which to cover themselves and these were spread about in a way that left each to fend for himself. They were headed south and also west, which extended their long night. For fourteen hours, they were hurled deep into the night, huddled and shivering. No one could sleep and yet hardly a word was spoken about their shared condition. It was a night of forced intimacy, mostly with strangers. They lay uncomfortably, listening only to the breathing around them and to the grumbling and grunts of those who turned to reach for blankets and tried their best to find an agreeable position.

The helicopter had taken them from the roof of The Tubes to a clearing in the forest. The trip, which, at the time, seemed like an eternity, now seemed like a just short hop compared to the second leg of their journey. Out the windows of the helicopter, they had seen few if any lights on the ground. Where they landed, there was a light blanket of snow on the ground. The area had been chosen carefully. It was lightly wooded so that an area for take-off might be cleared without too much trouble. This also allowed the jet to be hidden among trees without too much risk of it being observed from the air. The jet now awaited them on a makeshift runway. As they climbed down from the helicopter, they were buffeted by the wind created by the rotors. None were dressed for the near-freezing weather. Their coats were all still checked at The Tubes. They had been marched a hundred yards or so to the waiting jet and once aboard, took off within a matter of minutes at a terrifying rate and seemingly straight up. Their night was a strange constellation of breathing and snoring around them, mixed with raw fear and cold sweat, the faint glow of lighted cigarettes in the front of the cabin, with low voices in a language none could identify and the occasional dream for those lucky enough. While we at home were just learning of the attack, the captives were nearing their destination, although they could not have known it.

In the predawn, they began their descent to a tropical island. They touched down and the hostages were prodded out of the plane. In the semi-darkness could be seen red volcanic soil at the edge of the tarmac and beyond that, lush vegetation. The air was balmy, a bad sign at five AM. Several of the hostages were from Florida and they would soon experience heat and humidity of an intensity far greater than they had experienced at home. The group was herded into a camouflaged troop transport truck and driven out a dirt road that tunneled into the jungle. The captors were still wearing hoods. "That means they intend to release us." someone said. Coming with the very first sun rays, these were the first words that anyone dared speak about the new reality they were facing.

How the Captives Were Met

Their destination was a concrete block building painted a dull green, standing under a canopy of tall trees. The forest floor was shady all around. The captives were brought into the main room which looked like it might once have been a mess hall, as there was a kitchen behind a counter and tables and chairs were shoved to one side the room. The few windows were above eye level and there was no view of the outside. Mattresses were laid out on the floor with a sleeping bag on each one. The captives slept through the morning.

That afternoon, they sat at two picnic tables, side by side, and each was served a meal of rice and red beans on a tin plate. While they were eating, a hooded man addressed them in perfect English with just a trace of a French accent. "You are guests here and we expect you to behave accordingly. Your lives are not in danger. You will be provided with everything you need. There are bathrooms and showers in the building. Anyone who tries to escape will be dealt with harshly. Otherwise you are free to amuse yourselves as you see fit. That's all you need to know for now. Enjoy your stay." Then he added "Just so you know…Yes, we threw away the helicopter, but we still have the jet. We can use the jet. I hope the service onboard has met with your high standards."

"Who *are* you?" someone shouted.

"I thought you might be intelligent enough to know that you are not here to ask questions."

Afterwards, he approached the First Engineer with a slight bow. "Good morning, Mr. Forzley. By the way, it is none of my business, but I am curious. What kind of name is Forzley?"

"Lebanese".

This produced a quizzical tilt of the head from the terrorist. He knew that race can be a delicate issue for Americans. He himself was a bit darker than Victor Forzley, but he was not Black.

"I'm half Black, half Lebanese." Forzley added. He studied his captor, but could not extract much information. He could see only snapping black eyes behind the hood and they seemed to flash when their owner seemed pleased with himself.

"Certainly, no offense. In any case, good morning, Mr. Forzley. I have brought something to cheer you up, my very good friend. Read here" he said, holding a copy of the New York Times in one hand and smacking it with the other. They think we are in Pakistan. Hah! Like me, you are an engineer and engineers observe with precision. Therefore, I think you know differently."

Victor Forzley answered him. "I have no idea how you know that, but yes I am an engineer, an electrical engineer. What about yourself?"

"Likewise."

"I studied at Cal Tech. Where were you educated?"

"Ah. Ah. Too many questions. Suppose you answer mine. What can you deduce about our current position?"

"Alright. By my watch, the sun reaches its highest altitude here 10 hours after it does so on the West coast of America; which puts us about 3 hours East of Pakistan. Also, based on the hours of light and dark, we are quite a bit South of there as well. We moved from eight hours of light and sixteen of dark in California to just over twelve hours of light here. So, we are just South of the equator. I think we might be in Indonesia"

"You are reasonably close, my friend. So much for your CIA and FBI, those agents of 'the greatest nation on Earth', as you like to call yourselves. They have no idea where we are. Don't you wish you could tell them? Anyway, I'm so glad we had this chance to chat. Now give me your watch."

The Gentleman took off his hood. "There is no further use for this. We are now out of the range of American cameras." And with that, he left them and went into a back room.

The nineteen were left alone in the barren room, sitting on mattresses or else pacing. There was nothing to do. Then, by unspoken agreement, they pulled some mattresses into a circle and the introductions began. The weariness of the last day had broken through their natural reticence, and they were ready to join forces, to see what everyone brought to the table

Earlier, when they were all sitting in the helicopter, waiting on the roof of The Tubes, some had had a dim awareness of gunfire below, gunfire that could be heard just barely above the whirring of the blades. When introducing themselves, some instinctively referred to their companions left behind at the disco in the past tense. They appeared a motley group, drawn from many walks of life. Quite a few had money as it had been the terrorist's intention to select them on that basis.

Among the captives, and in no particular order, was a biker, a man named Arnold Powers, fifty years of age. He was not tall, maybe five-eight, but powerfully built. He was well beyond his fighting days, as was evident from his thick and pure white crew cut. He had come from a broken and violent home. He had a father, long dead, whom he had barely known. He stood and addressed the group. "Fellow travelers, my name is Arnie, Arnie Powers. They call me the Great White on account of this [rubbing his hair]. I'm the President of the Knuckle Draggers Motorcycle Club, Fresno, California. As you can see, I've been captured while displaying my full colors. Sounds like something you'd here on one of them nature shows, don't it?" With that, he turned around so all could see the back of his black leather jacket, where an ape was swinging a battle axe with one hand and mace with the other. Across the top, it read Knuckle Draggers, and across the bottom, Fresno, CA. "Back in the day, I was the Sergeant-at-Arms of that same outfit and I can tell you sure enough, I laid out more than a few dudes in my time. Sergeant-at-Arms is the title I'm most proud of, but it's a little fancy for everyday use, so let's go with the Great White." At the time of his capture, Arnie Powers was a very wealthy man. He was one of the biggest manufacturers and dealers of methamphetamine on the west coast. Arnie was a true silverback in the motorcycle world, not because he was the toughest or the most violent, but because he was one of the smartest. He was wearing designer jeans and a pair of ostrich skin cowboy boots, the heels of which brought him up a couple of needed inches. "I came to that ski resort with my lawyer." He added. "She'll introduce herself. Also with us were two of my best men. They were good dudes, wherever they are now."

The Sergeant-at-Arms' Lawyer was Dolores Diaz. She was thirty-five. Dolores stood five-foot eight and would have been even with the Sergeant-at-Arms had it not been for his cowboy boots. She had flowing and shining black hair, and it was only her hardness that kept her from being beautiful. She remained seated. "I'm Dolores Diaz. Mr. Powers is my only client and I like to think I have helped him become a successful businessman. I have many connections within law enforcement. I have family both in L.A. and in Guanajuato, Mexico." The Lawyer managed the Sergeants-at-Arms' outstanding charges as well as bribes necessary to run a profitable drug business. There were also things she could not mention, such as the way she had helped him silence a would-be blackmailer who had threatened to reveal to the Great White's wife, his occasional gay activity. The four of them who had made the trip, that is the Lawyer, the Sergeant-at-Arms and two of his henchmen, had some interesting home movies.

"So…I'm Martin Pelli." said a dark-haired, thin-lipped man of about forty-five. "I own Lansing Nutraceuticals. We are a major distributor of vitamins and food supplements." He stood brushing down the sleeves of his green-gold Armani silk suit. "I'm still trying to work the kinks out from that plane ride. I can't say I like the accommodations so far."

The Sergeant-at-Arms piped up. "You may be used to flying gold or platinum; but right now, pal, you're in sheet metal class."

"Have you ever had your DNA tested? You look like you might have a good bit of Neanderthal in you."

"Who was that bird I saw you with on the dance floor?"

"I'll thank you to mind your own business."

The Sergeant-at-Arms smiled and, as his aim was to upset the Executive rather than to have the last word, he said no more. After that the Executive was silent, too, for truly, the woman in question was not his wife.

Next to introduce himself was a Physiologist. "Evet St. Rob, Gainesville, Florida. Recently, I retired from research and teaching to become a writer. A few years back, I broke my leg and did some damage to my knee. My surgeon told me never to ski again and I've taken his advice. So why was I at the Mount Lasser Resort? First, it's a great place to find solitude and write. I came with a laptop, not skis. Second, Roland White, the architect who designed The Tubes was my college roommate and I had always wanted to see the place. But the most important reason I was there is that Ian Underwood whose band you all heard that night…was it really only *last* night? Anyway, Ian Underwood is a stage name and Ian is my son."

"Hah hah! He *thinks* I'm his son, but he doesn't know for sure. A man never does. You all know me. The Chameleons are based out of L.A. I left the rest of the band back at the club. I hope they are OK, just as they must hope that I'm OK. And that's the very last serious statement you'll ever hear from me." The Musician wore a green and white jester's suit. He had just changed into it for the start of the second set. He leaned his head down and shook the bells of his fool's cap. He had an epic beard and although he was good-sized, he had the manner of an imp, always singing and whistling. He would quickly get to know all of the other captives.

There was also a Psychologist named Claudia Talmadge, aged forty-five from Knoxville, Tennessee. Claudia was a no nonsense type. She wore a white blouse and pleated skirt. She explained that she was a school psychologist and how she and her husband were on a ski trip while his parents watched their two teen-agers.

There were two Engineers. The first spoke up. "Victor Forzley, here." Victor was a slim and serious man, aged forty. "There were four of us on a ski trip. We were all members of Alpha Phi Alpha fraternity back at Drew University. We've had a few reunions over the years. With me I have my fellow omega-man Marcus McCabe. I am the senior member of the group." The Second Engineer cut in. "Now just a darn minute there, young fella. You may be the oldest by a couple of months, but you were not the first to graduate. You see, folks, Victor required an extra year at Drew, a *remedial* year, if I may be frank." Marcus let out a hearty laugh. He was stocky with a couple of extra pounds, glad-handed, and a bit of a bragger.

Carol Osterberg, aged 68, was Heiress to the family fortune of Osterberg Farms, which was at one time the largest dairy farming and distributing business in the country. "I'm Carol Osterberg. Some of you may remember me from the old TV ads for Carol's Custard. I was little Carol. Today, my husband and I have a glass-blowing studio in Asheville, North Carolina. Ted was skiing while I went to hear the band at The Tubes. I can only imagine how worried he must be." The Heiress was someone who jealously guarded her privacy. She and her husband had a hippie vibe that was just a little at odds with the Midwestern values of her family.

Ken Holliman, aged 78, was a physician, a neurologist. "Hey, hi, how are you? I'm Ken. I'm a physician and a researcher. I was at the Mount Lasser Resort for a little ski trip slash scientific meeting that I organize from time to time. There were seven of us. The others were/ are younger people whom I have trained over the years. I don't ski. Do I look like I ski? Come on. I'm no spring chicken. Here's what we do, OK. Everyone presents their recent work in the morning and then they ski the rest of the day. They enjoy skiing. And that's how we maintain our network of research collaborators." The Physician had a white mustache and he wore a bow tie. He added "I told the head honcho terrorist back at the disco that I have a serious cardiac arrhythmia, you know, an irregular heartbeat, and I told him that I would be in great danger without my medication. He just grinned at me. I said, 'How can you hope to get ransom from my family if I'm dead?' 'So, you have money.' he says and pushes me along towards the helicopter. That was my mistake. Or maybe it didn't make any difference. Who knows about these things?"

Next to be heard was Richard Neudeck, Lieutenant Colonel, US Navy, retired. "I was a Navy pilot. I flew just about everything you can imagine. Now I'm climbing mountains. This past summer, I was part of a team that climbed the North face of the Matterhorn. I ski as often as I can. I left a buddy back at the lodge." The Navy Pilot was in his early fifties, a typical military sort; small, compact and athletic, a man of few words, an adrenaline junkie. He was keeping a secret from the other captives. Navy doctors had installed, in his calf, a state-of-the-art tracking device that cost a fortune and was unavailable to civilians. The device sent out a signal, once every fifteen minutes and its battery was recharged by physical activity.

Sitting next to the Navy Pilot was Elytra Noll, who was a bartender working at The Tubes at the time of the raid. She didn't get up; she was sleepy. She just smiled and turned her head to the side. "I'm Elytra. You know me from the bar." There was a pause before someone said, "Elytra is an unusual name." "*These* are elytra" she said and with that, she took off her earrings and passed them around the room. "These earrings are made from the hard, outer, protective wings of the jewel beetle. They were given to me by my mother; she got them in Bangkok. The deep black with green iridescent highlights really speak to me. They're called elytra, just like me." The Bartender's hair was dyed black, with iridescent blue and green overtones. At twenty-eight, she looked a little bookish and a little wild at the same time. She had lived in a number of exotic locations. Her tip jar at The Tubes had read 'Give us the money, Lebowski.' She had been captured in her tuxedo work uniform.

A woman in her early forties stood up. "I'm Lauren Campbell. I'm from North Florida. My husband Rick and I are both teachers. We're also water skiers and in the summers, we run a water ski camp. At the end of each season we help the kids put on a show to raise money for charity. Rick and I thought we'd splurge on a snow ski trip while my parents watch our three kids. I left Rick back at the nightclub."

A woman in her late twenties spoke up. "My name is Petra Martens and I'm an event planner. Two summers ago, I organized a wedding at the Mount Lasser Resort and ever since, I've wanted to come back to ski." Lauren noticed her slight accent. Petra smiled back at her. "My family moved from the Netherlands to the States when I was twelve."

The next turn fell to a man in his thirties who sat with his face in his hands, blond hair hanging down. After a minute, Claudia, the Psychologist said "Do you want to introduce yourself? You don't have to." He raised his face for a moment and shook his head no. Fulton Hale, the Ski Bum was tall, slim and athletic. He had a tanned and handsome face with thick blond eyelashes and a downward, guilty cast. His was a face that radiated weakness. He was disliked on sight by most of the other captives. He looked like the sun hurt his eyes although it was not bright in the room. He also looked like he needed a drink. He gave the disquieting impression of someone who, purely out of weakness, could put himself in a position of danger. At Mount Lasser he had given some ski lessons and done a little hustling.

Next came three twenty-somethings. Ryan Sinclair had red hair and a goatee. He described himself as a Programmer, based out of Chicago. He and two others were on assignment with a firm in Portland, Oregon and they made the trip south to Mount Lasser. Sunny Fine was a Ski Jumper and Olympic hopeful. Hi Makanudo was a college basketball player whose family owned a chain of sushi restaurants in Southern California.

After waiting her turn until last, a stern-looking woman stood and announced defiantly, "I am Mrs. White." With that, she placed her hands on her hips. Mrs. White was in her sixties. She had thick, steel-gray hair that was cut short and she might have been called handsome except that she invariably turned men off with her abrupt and disapproving manner. She turned her head and glared at each of the other captives. After a pause, the Psychologist asked. "Could you tell us a little more about yourself, Mrs. White?" "Well, I suppose I don't see why not. My husband Cliff and I live in Fairfield, Connecticut. He is the one who wanted to come to the ski resort. He sails, he skis and he plays handball. I do *not* do those things. And I certainly would never have set foot in that awful nightclub except to tell Cliff to come back to the room. And now here we are, all of us, in this incredibly undignified position." The Psychologist asked, "How did you spend your time while your husband was skiing?" "Well, if you really must know, I caught up on my letter writing." "Letter writing, really?" the Physiologist couldn't help asking. "Do you send them by pony express? I don't know if you've heard, but we have email now." "I do *not* use computers and I resent your smart –aleck tone."

Cast of Characters

The Sergeant-at-Arms - Arnie Powers

The Lawyer – Dolores Del Rio

The Executive – Martin Pelli

The Physiologist - Evet St. Rob

The Musician – Ian Underwood

The Psychologist – Claudia Talmadge

The First Engineer – Victor Forzley

The Second Engineer – Marcus McCabe

The Heiress – Carol Osterberg

The Physician – Ken Holliman

The Navy Pilot - Richard Neudeck

The Bartender - Elytra Noll

Lauren Campbell

The Event Planner – Petra Martens

The Ski Bum – Fulton Hale

The Programmer – Ryan Sinclair

Hi Makanudo

The Ski Jumper - Sunny Fine

Mrs. White

How the Captives Passed the Time

At breakfast, on the second morning, the meal was the same red beans and rice. It was clear to the captives that it would be the same every day, with just one meal to last the day. That only made sense because they were in a remote location and those foods could be stored dry. The nineteen were crowded into two picnic tables. As his meal was being ladled out, the Physiologist stood and addressed the Gentleman. "I'm a little disappointed, sir. Where is the French cuisine? I was expecting maybe beef bourguignon with couscous and a nice bottle of Mouton Cadet."

"Instead, you get this!" the Gentleman said calmly as he thrust the butt of his rifle into the Physiologist's gut. The Physiologist doubled over, then stood up and took a half step toward the Gentleman before thinking better of it.

The Gentleman smiled. "That was your mistake sir. I am not French. I merely learned French before I learned English. That little bit of physical reinforcement that I just gave you will certainly serve to remind you that I am not French. You should thank me for that. And now, I must leave. I hope that everyone will enjoy his meal under these less-than-ideal conditions. Good day."

After, the Gentleman was gone, the Sergeant-at-Arms leaned in and said, "I like your style, bro."

But after that, the remainder of the meal was silent, embarrassingly so because all realized they should be getting to know one another.

After he finished eating, the Sergeant-at-Arms announced, "Hey everybody, I know a little ice-breaker to get the conversation started." With that, he stood up, put his boot on the bench and began to roll up his pant leg, revealing an angry scar that ran from the outside of his knee down toward his ankle. "This right here happened in a fight with some Angels who were somewhere they were not supposed to be. While I was punching out this one dude, another Angel who was already down, managed to crawl up and get his knife into me. I lost a lot of blood, partly because I couldn't tend to it right away, being a little bit busy as I was. However, there was no lasting damage other than this nice little souvenir."

"No nerves cut? You seem to move about normally." observed the Physician.

"The doctor told me that when a wound runs the length of a limb, there's not so much likelihood that nerves will be cut. Anyway, Knuckle Draggers won that fight and a dude on the other side got killed in the process. I was charged as an accessory to murder and I ended up doing a year for that. Proudest day of my life."

"I'm a little surprised," added the Physician. "But I see the scar and I see that you have full use of your leg. I'm not in the habit of trying to argue with reality."

Claudia Talmadge, the Psychologist, kept the ball rolling by showing a small round scar on her arm. "When I was six, my Dad's boss and his wife came over for dinner. Before dinner, we walked around the yard to show them our fruit trees. I was a big show-off at the time. My husband says I still am. I said to them, 'Look, look what I can do.' and I tumbled down a small embankment. Only I went further than I meant to and landed in the rosebushes. I got an enormous number of Band-Aids and cried all the way through dinner. My parents say the boss and his wife were charmed. I don't remember it too well. But I have this reminder that humility is always the best policy. Who else has a scar to show?"

The Physiologist was next. "This is not exactly a scar, more of a home-made tattoo. Here, take a look." He pulled down his left eyelid to reveal a blue pen mark that had been left under the skin. "I was about twelve. I was over at a friend's house. I say 'friend', but you know how it is with boys that age. We were as much rivals as friends. We were in the den watching Davey Crocket on TV. Born on a mountaintop in Tennessee, greenest state in the land of the free. Davey Crocket and Red Stick were in a knife fight. Red Stick had his knife an inch from

Boone's face and Boone had a hold of his wrist and was fighting hard to hold him back. Eventually Daniel Boone won the fight and spared Red Stick's life, allowing a treaty to take place. Suddenly my buddy jumped me only instead of a Bowie knife, he had a ball-point pen in his hand. We wrestled for a while and then my hand slipped off of his wrist. The pen stuck in my eyelid and the result is what you see."

Lauren Campbell showed a scar on her thigh. It was smooth and shiny, shaped like a football or one of those patches in a piece of plywood. "I was about ten when I got this. I tripped on the back stoop with a bottle of milk in my hand. There was a shard of curved glass imbedded in the wound. That was back in the 1950s, back when milk was delivered to your backdoor by a milkman and came in quart bottles made of thick glass."

The Second Engineer rolled up his sleeve. "Let's show them the Omegas, brother." The First Engineer also rolled up his sleeve and the two displayed their Omega scars, each on the outside of the shoulder, square on the deltoid. "You are lookin at the mark of the Omega Psi Phi Fraternity. A lot of big people have it. Michael Jordan does; Count Basie did. There were four of us back at the ski lodge. We were all at Drew University together."

"That's a brand, isn't it?"

"Yes, it is."

"Did it hurt?"

"Oh yes, ma'am, it did. All you get is a little ice to numb your arm. You just got to man-up. That's all."

Then the First Engineer called attention to a small white scar below his lower lip. "This one has a story. See, I had my Wonder years, you know, when you grow to ninety percent of your adult height and you need all the goodness of Wonder Bread? I had those years Connecticut."

"Victor came up in the suburbs, y'all." the Second Engineer laughed.

"You got a problem with that? We had snow where I grew up. Marcus couldn't handle snow; he'd be cryin to his Momma. Marcus wouldn't know which end of a snow shovel to use. We had this big hill, behind the neighborhood, and we'd be runnin down it on our sleds all day long until the dinner bell. At the bottom of that hill was a stone wall with an opening where there must have been a gate at one time. A whole mess of us would start together at the top; but there was only room enough for one to make it through that gate. That's what made the whole thing interesting. There was surely no better feeling than passing through the gate after forcing someone else to crash into the wall. Four or five times over the years, somebody put a tooth through their lip either from an elbow or else from the stone wall itself. I'm proud to be a member of that club. Here is my scar. I wore like a badge of honor all through my comin-up years."

The Bartender said, "I've got something to show you; but it's not a scar." And with that, she discreetly pulled up the back of her tuxedo shirt to reveal a tattoo across her shoulder blades."

"Well!" intoned Mrs. White. "I certainly didn't come here to see a striptease show."

"This is *not* a strip show…"

"You may be excused if you like, Mrs. White." said the Physiologist.

"Gladly." she said and stomped off to the other side of the room.

Everyone crowded in for a better look. Over the Bartender's left shoulder blade was a jewel beetle just taking off from a flowering branch. Over the center of her back was a beetle in free flight. Its delicate flying wings were rendered in exquisite detail. Its body and its protective wings were burnished and looked like a pair of oars just leaving the water. On the right shoulder, another jewel beetle was just landing on another branch. "I had this done in Bangkok. The deep black color with green iridescent highlights really speaks to me. And those hard, outer wings, they're called elytra, just like me. You see I need the protection of a hard shell just as much as the beetle does."

The Musician chimed in "Why is that, Elytra? If you don't mind my asking, that is."

"Well, I'll tell you just a little, sweetie. I was abandoned as a child. I grew up in a beautiful Victorian house. The house was always full of hippies. I remember my parents' drug parties. My mother had inherited the house free and clear and it was worth a lot. By the time I was twelve, they had mortgaged it to the hilt all for lavish spending, and dope, of course. When the bank foreclosed on us, we moved from one dingy apartment to another. The money had run out and my Dad took off. My mother was a good woman, and she loved me in her way, but she couldn't take care of herself, much less me. Five years later, she died of an overdose and I finished high school living with a family friend."

"I'm really sorry," said the Musician. "And now I feel like I've intruded."

"Oh, don't worry. You're hardly the first I've told."

"Elytra, I know you!" the Physiologist called out. "Something rang a bell when I first heard your voice the other day. See, I have this useless ability to recognizes voices. Usually when someone calls me on the phone, I can recognize them from just the first word or two, even if I have met the person only once." She squinted at him. "Anyway, I know you from the coffee shop at the VA hospital in Denver. Final answer."

"Yes, that's right, I worked there for a couple of months."

"Well, I stopped in for coffee. I was on a trip, visiting a research lab there. But you didn't look the way you do now. Your hair was different. See, it's all about the voice."

"Your hair is always changing, but I still don't remember you."

"You told me you were there visiting your Dad. In light of what you just said, how did that go?"

"Not well. He's unreachable. He's a druggie. He's a man with an IQ of a hundred and fifty-five who works in a gift shop at Rocky Mountain National Park. That's what he's done with his life. And that's when he's working, which isn't often."

"I'm really sorry. But hey, do you remember this? Later in that same day, we were both in that little alcove where they keep the vending machines, not far from the coffee shop. In comes some loud mouthed crusty bastard lecturing everyone in sight about The Lord. I remember him looking right at you and shouting, 'What part of 'Thou shall not' do they not understand?' And I asked him 'Sir, are you aware that some people object to religion on moral grounds?' You held up two fingers in front of his face and told him 'Two, right here in this room.' After that, he left without saying another word. Sweet."

"You know what, I do remember that. Yes, I do. Thank you."

After a moment, the Navy Pilot spoke up. "Here is a scar you can barely see." He pulled up his shirt and traced a path of about five inches across his abdomen. Some could see it; some could not. "Three years ago, I donated a kidney to my sister."

"How is your sister doing?" asked the Psychologist.

"She rejected it. She is gone."

"Oh."

After an uncomfortable silence, the Navy Pilot, who was not known for being diplomatic, continued. "My point is that the scar is nearly gone. I have older scars that are completely gone or almost gone. Here" he said [rolling up his pant leg. "is where I had surgery for an ACL tear. High school football. Gone. Here, look at my thumb. This is another example. I was twelve, maybe thirteen, messing around melting and burning some plastic bags. Boy Scout camp. I got drops of burning plastic all over my thumb. For years I had an ugly, bumpy scar about a half inch wide running from the bottom of my thumb nail to where my thumb joins the wrist. Now look, there is nothing. There are other examples."

"I don't see anything. Maybe a faint little white mark, shaped like the letter Y."

"The point is, I have remarkable healing powers; my scars disappear and they do so quickly. You never know when such a thing might come in handy, especially in a situation like the one we face here."

"What the hell is that supposed to mean?" demanded the Executive.

"That one's on a need-to-know basis, brother. That's all I can tell you right now." The Navy Pilot seemed pleased with himself in a childish kind of way.

A Short Book of Dreams

Early on the third morning, an off-key bugle jolted the nineteen. Some were already up and about. Some had already used the bathroom, which provided a toilet and sink, tooth brushes and tooth paste. Some were sleepily contemplating the limits of their new universe; a large and open room, four walls of concrete block painted a dull gray-green. High on one wall, small dirty windows let in only a small amount of light and so it was dark, even at the peak of day. Mattresses covered the floor on one side and on the other were tables where one of the captors was ladling steaming glop into bowls. Another captor kicked the Physician and then the Physiologist who were still sleeping.

As they finished eating, the Psychologist spoke up over the grumbling. "We've all shown our scars and today, we need another way to occupy ourselves, some way to fill the time. I lead a dream group back in Tennessee. We meet once a month in my living room and each of us recalls a dream or two and we discuss them. We could do that here. I think it would be a good way to get to know each other."

There was some interest among the group, so the Psychologist continued. "Before we get started, there is one thing I want to emphasize. That is the principle that 'only the dreamer knows'. Of course, we can speculate about the meaning of someone else's dream, but all of our speculations are what we psychologists call 'projection'. That essentially means putting our own point of view onto someone else. So, to reinforce that principle, when you comment on someone else's dream, please phrase it like this: 'If this were my dream...or, in my version of the dream...'. Having said that, does anyone have a dream they would like to share?"

The First Engineer said "Sure. I had a dream last night. I was standing at the top of a great ziggurat of oven-fired bricks looking out over an infinite and arid plain. The ziggurat rose in five stages and I stood at the top of a grand staircase which descended, through two great arches, all the way to the desert floor. At my back was a shrine, finished with fine brick, laid in a herringbone pattern. I looked toward a far range of mountains, blue and purple in the distance. At the top of the tallest mountain was set an enormous sapphire of so deep a blue that it promised of eternity. A single ray of light from that sapphire reached me through the gloom of pre-dawn and I knew at once that I must reach it at all costs. To my amazement, I found myself completely free to leave the ziggurat and, passing among Sumerian priests, I began to descend the staircase, through the two arches and along a passageway that was decorated with touches of red and blue and gold. When I got to the bottom, I saw that the plain I would have to cross was not an ordinary desert floor, but instead a labyrinth of mud walls that stretched to the horizon and that even a lifetime would not be enough to reach my goal."

The Psychologist said "Your dream is dripping with vivid images. Tell us what it means to you."

"I think it's straight-forward. We're all trapped here and we may never find our way out."

"True enough" said the Psychologist. "And what does the sapphire mean to you?"

"Not the next life, if that's where you're headed. For me, it's satisfaction, some sign that my life has a purpose. And how can I pursue that goal when I'm trapped here?"

The Physiologist spoke up. "I had a dream about being trapped, too. I was vaguely aware of a black planet, a shadow planet, unknown to astronomers because it has no mass and no gravity. The shadow planet inhabited, nearly filled, the space between the moon and Mars and its surface was completely covered in the soft, dry wings of countless bats. Suddenly, as if in response to some secret signal, the bats began to swoop down to Earth in a single black ribbon. They covered the Earth and they stripped the trees bare of fruit and then they ate the leaves and grasses and finally there was nothing green left alive." The Bartender cringed a little as she listened.

"There were only a few of us left and we hid from the bats in a concrete bunker in the shape of a cube, a couple of hundred feet on a side. In our dark misery, we could hear the bats attacking the ventilation grates and we knew it was only a matter of time. I woke up, covered in sweat. I didn't want to go back to sleep, didn't want to return to that world."

"Your dream is a little different than mine." said the First Engineer. "We're both trapped, we're all trapped in this alien place. For me it's tantalizing because I can't be where I want to be. But for you, it sounds like pure torment. For you, the worst is already here."

"That's just me. My wife always tells me I take things harder than I need to."

The Psychologist asked, "Who else had a dream they would like to share?"

There were no other offers, so the Physiologist spoke up again. "While we were on the plane and while we were here last night, I had a whole series of dreams, some rambling, some troubling. I can tell you as many as you'd like to hear."

A couple of heads nodded.

"In the first dream, I was with my Dad riding the train into Manhattan. I was eighteen years old. We were both going to work. He was wearing a business suit and I had on jeans and boots for my summer construction job, one he had gotten for me. We passed through Westchester County, taking a slow curve with the tracks on a raised bed of gravel. All around us, sumacs leaned in, reaching for a little sunlight. As we came to Mamaroneck, the town where my Dad was raised, the conductor came by to punch our tickets. The conductor, who greeted my Dad by name, was noticeably subdued. As soon as he left, my Dad, who is too kind to have said this to the man's face, told me, 'in high school, that guy thought he was better than me. Now he knows he isn't'."

The Bartender asked, "Did you go through the same thing that your Dad did? Did you struggle for respect with the other boys?"

"Our situations were the same in some ways; different in others. We were both overlooked, underestimated and sometimes picked on by bullies, loudmouths and louts. And now that I'm older than my Dad was in the dream, I share his satisfaction in knowing that I've had some success in life and also in knowing that a lot of those guys who thought they were so cool in junior high school ended up going nowhere; jobs where you wear your first name on your shirt, alcohol, divorce. But the reasons we each had a hard time were different. I was an introvert. I was a kid who stared at the ground a lot. I never knew what was going on. He, on the other hand, skipped three grades. So, he had the disadvantage of being younger that his classmates."

The Psychologist prompted the group "Who wants to go next?" There was no answer, so the physiologist asked, "Well if no one else wants to talk, do you mind if I go on?" There was a little grumble of approval, so he continued. "Next, I had three dreams, in quick succession. They're short; all about my boys, who are grown now. In the first dream, Matthew, our older son, was on the run. He'd run afoul of the law. I didn't have all the details, but in some vague way, I knew he'd taken a moral stand, like many outlaws of legend. I was proud of him. Matthew had come upon a perfect way to hide. He'd become a bear and he was living in the wilds of Alaska. But he was still himself and he could still talk. I thought, 'I have to go up there and bring him a pickup truckload of fish.'"

"Your son is Matthew, not Ian?" asked the Programmer.

"No, Matthew is our older son; Ian is our younger son. Ian Underwood is a stage name. His real name is David St. Rob.

"What does the bear mean to you, other than that he eats fish?" asked the Psychologist.

"Changing into a bear was Matthew's escape from the chase; he didn't have to keep running."

"Of course. I wonder if there is something in your life you are running from."

"I wish I could run way from here! But also, I've always dreamed of safe havens, places to be alone with my thoughts. And I'll tell you about some of those dreams, too, if you're interested."

"Well first, let's see who else has a dream." But there were still no volunteers, so the Physiologist went on. "In the second dream about our boys, Matthew was small and David, who is really Ian, was in our arms. We were on a trip and changing planes in Antarctica. In the gloom of perpetual night, we stepped down from the tarmac toward a dark river where we all climbed aboard a speed boat with high steel sides. While we are waiting to depart, Matthew decided he wanted to go swimming and jumped over the gunwale in his winter coat. The sides of the boat were high and I couldn't reach him. Had to jump in myself and lift him up to Renee who pulled him out of the water. We were wringing out our jackets and shivering as the boat lurched forward. We passed finger islands, black as obsidian. They had gleaming facets that quivered like the cut face of a flan custard when our wake was thrown against them. Overhead, the stars were growing like ice crystals. The lights of the terminal were only a distant constellation.

"Why do you suppose Matthew jumped out of the boat?" asked the Bartender. "In my dream, it would be taking a chance, leaping without looking."

"When he was small, especially, I used to worry that he underestimated the dangers of the world. I think that must be why I had him jump. Now, in the third dream, I was telling my brother-in-law how our boys were two exotic insects that we brought back from a trip to South America. He said, 'I can see how David is no ordinary housefly. He's a little bigger, sleeker and lighter in color.' I said, 'We took him home in a bottle with tiny holes in the cap.' I also told him how we had found Matthew, who was a butterfly with blue undersides, lying on the ground. We didn't have another bottle, so I held him between cupped hands. He must have been cold because he immediately came to life.'

"I went on to tell my brother-in-law how I had taken the two boys to the back entrance of a troll's woodshop. The steps were made of stacked lumber. I had one boy on each shoulder. I was out of breath before reaching the top step. Matthew was to make wooden candle sticks for his woodshop class. The troll said the wood alone would cost two dollars. That seemed like a lot, so we must have been somewhere back in the past. Matthew whispered, 'I don't think we can afford two dollars'. I whispered back, 'I just want to see how they are made. We can make our own from wood we have in the garage.' After that, I drove the boys home in our old green Volvo with no steering wheel. I had a vice-grip on the bolt where the steering wheel should have been attached. Driving was difficult. I had to abandon the car and walk the last few blocks. On the way, we encountered an old biddy sweeping the street in front of her house. She took one look at Ian and said she didn't want any insects near her house."

When he was done, the Psychologist remarked "Such intricate dream symbols - I am intrigued by what seems to be the omnipresence of your sons. How do you understand that?"

"Well, they are the most important parts of my life - besides my wife! This makes me feel that the dream is an important dream. It is interesting that in order to be safe, my son morphed into a bear."

The Physiologist added, "I've got just one more dream if you have time." And as there were no objections, he went ahead. "This last one is an example of another type of safe haven dream. This is one of my barroom dreams. I have them all the time. This time I was driving deep into the middle of the night. Blackness was all around. My headlights created just a few feet of roadway that kept rising to meet my wheels and without that miracle I might have plunged into the abyss. The road signs were grimy and smeared with starlight. I passed a wrecker with lights flashing up and down its boom and it looked like the greedy jaws of a lantern fish making its way along the ocean floor. A splash of headlight up one side of an overpass made a top-heavy and precarious piece of modern sculpture. Exit signs beckoned, each promising a different world and finally, I took one. It was pitch black. All I could do was follow the tail lights in front of me. Then, miles from any highway, those headlights disappeared and the road ended. I got out and walked around until I found a dirt path and that led me to a log cabin. The entryway had no door and I passed inside by stepping over a sleeping giant. Mountain elves with beards to their knees ran back and forth over the bar top, carrying frosty pitchers of beer. In a black box attached to the ceiling and behind the bar, the Doors were playing. I watched the furious energy of the miniature figures as the music filled the room with danger. Next, I was sitting in a little tin bar in Central America with a drink of rum and cane juice. Outside, the sound of insects was overpowering. Drinks were served by a three-toed sloth lying across the bar who would wait for you to put a coin onto a plate before pushing a little glass full of clear and thick liquor your way. It took all the effort he could muster just to keep his eyes open. I felt a great calm and mystery in there. It's always the same in these dreams. The barroom is a holy place, a place of refuge and escape, a place of mystery and adventure, a place to go from time to time where I can stand outside of time."

The first engineer piped in, "Wow, your road ended. In my dream version, the end of the road sounds terrifying, sounds like death. The walk on the dirt road is the after-life. Does that resonate for you?"

"Not exactly. For me, the dirt road, the road less taken, is being free in my dreams to explore unknown worlds."

The Psychologist remarked, "How curious that bars are a place of holiness! Tell us more about what holiness is for you. And I am full of wonder about that sleeping giant, too. What do giants symbolize for you?"

"Well, first, about the barrooms; I'm not a drinker. I'll have one or two socially. I'm pretty average that way. But drinking was strongly looked down upon in my family growing up, almost forbidden. Back in the Great Depression, my mother's family provided meals to the families of cousins whose fathers drank away their paychecks. As a child, drinking was a world of forbidden mystery to me."

"And what about the giant?"

"The giant is dangerous. Don't wake him up."

The Sergeant-at-Arms cut in, "Speaking of barrooms, I could use a cold beer right now. But this ain't no tavern we find ourselves in. Hey, I had a dream last night, too. I'm on the beach in Italy, a little sandy spot between rock outcroppings, very private. I see a gray streak in the sky and at first, it looks like the vapor trail of a jet. But, as it approaches, as it gets closer and closer, I can see it is not gray at all, but is instead made out of every color you can imagine. Finally, when it gets close enough, I can see that it is, in fact, a great ribbon of cars and trucks flying through the sky, just as if there were some kind of highway up there. I'm thinking, 'Oh my god, they're going to plunge into the sea once they realize where they are, once they stop believing'. Next thing I know, there is Jesus Christ himself, standing in the air beside a crystal chandelier and one by one, he called the rest of us to move up and stand beside him."

The Bartender said, "So you're still a believer."

"Well, I don't know about that. There's just some things you can never get entirely out of your system, if you know what I mean."

"I do know what you mean. But that also means you're still a believer. Don't get me wrong, that says something good about you."

"Well, this situation ain't good; we're gonna need a higher power."

The Programmer spoke up. "This is an old dream, but it's one that has stayed with me. I had just finished reading 'Sharpening My Sense of Mortality on the 12th of November' by A.M. Chaudhry and it moved me so much that I decided at once that I must meet the author. I don't think there is such a book. But even now, awake, I still *feel* like it's real. That's just the hangover of the dream working; I'm pretty sure it's not real. According to the book jacket, Mr. Chaudhry lived in Calcutta. As the dream starts, I'm one of three, headed to a computer science convention in Acapulco and I decide to book the extra leg to India. Chaudhry is a slippery fellow and all morning he is trying to make me forget my dream. He keeps diving into my subconscious and I keep pulling him out by the heel because I really enjoyed that dream. Next, I'm in Acapulco, in the Farmacia Gigante, wandering up and down the aisles, searching for Chaudhry. I know that he was quite popular on the literary scene, but not a best seller, so I would be a bit surprised to see him in a place like this. Harsh fluorescent lights were flickering and the people I encounter offer forced smiles. In the garish light, their teeth appear a bright yellow. In the book section, I find all kinds of romances and biographies of tabloid celebrities; what you might expect to find in a drug store. No A.M. Chaudhry. But, they do have an interesting old hardback about an economist who became a biologist after developing a rare liver disorder. It turns out that he did make an important discovery about that liver disease, but it did not impact his own case and it didn't save him. I stand there a long time, getting a good way through it. They also have a scientific textbook about iron toxicity, but I don't buy it because it was published in 1969 and is probably out of date. I'm beginning to think Mr. Chaudhry might be a figment of my imagination. When viewed from above, the book aisles form the shape of the letter S, with a disconnected piece making a comma after the S. I searched to find any significance in that. Back at the hotel, I find Rajah, one of my companions on the trip to Acapulco. He is sitting in the restaurant with a cup of tea. He is steaming. He tells me, 'Can you believe this? Can you believe this? I'm checking in to the hotel and the guy behind the desk asks me if I want a girl sent up to my room. This is a major hotel and he asks me that! So, I try politely to tell him no and he says I understand; you like boys. I will have a boy sent up. This seriously pisses me off.' After he cools down a bit, I tell him about my plan to go to India and find A.M. Chaudhry. This gets him all hot and bothered again. He tells me, 'In the time that I have known you, you have done many impulsive things, my friend, but this absolutely takes the cake. Calcutta is a very dangerous place. Do not appear on the street. Based on your appearance, you will be robbed. My advice to you is this; hire a driver at the airport and keep his services 24 hours a day until you return to the airport. This you can do very cheaply. What is the address?' I said, 'I don't know where he lives, other than Calcutta.' Rajah continues, 'And you don't even know if he is at home or even in-country. Chaudhry is a very common name. Do you know how many millions live in Calcutta? Unbelievable. Unbelievable.'"

"Very interesting", remarked the Psychologist. "Tell us about the whole 'hot and bothered' thing. In my dream that emotion was big."

"Well, in real life, Rajah is my friend from work. He is very proper, very cautious, and easily offended. So, the situation at the end fits him. That's how Rajah would react."

"But,", interrupted the Psychologist "Jung taught that all the people in the dream are parts of your own psyche. I wonder what is 'hot and bothered' in you.

"Are you kidding me? I am hot and bothered about being here right now!"

"And what about your sense of mortality?"

"I had this dream a couple of months ago, but yes, right now my sense of mortality is about as sharp as it needs to be. I don't need any help from Mr. Chaudhry."

A Second Day of Dreams

The following morning, the Psychologist asked again who had dreams to share, but only the Physiologist offered. "I had a whole series of dreams last night, all on the same theme of reliving the struggles I had trying to establish myself as a scientist. They all go back to my days as a grad student in a department that was full of stress and treachery.

"The first dream involves the chemical EDTA. Does anyone remember the role of EDTA in the O.J. Simpson case? [no answer]. EDTA is an anticoagulant and it's added to the blood drawn by the police for DNA testing; added in to prevent the blood from clotting. EDTA works by chelating calcium ions, by removing them. Without calcium, the blood cannot clot. The defense argued that O.J.'s blood that was said to be from the crime scene was really the taken from the sample drawn in the police station. Any sample taken in the police station would necessarily contain EDTA and the L.A. County Coroner's office could not state with absolute certainty that there was no EDTA in the sample in question. The Chief Coroner testified that sample from the crime scene had been tested and that a finding was made of several parts per million EDTA, so he couldn't rule out completely the possibility that the blood came from an EDTA tube drawn at the police station. But the Coroner made a serious error. The concentration of calcium in the blood is about two parts per *thousand*; thousand, not million. Just to be on the safe side, to be sure that all calcium has been removed, EDTA in the blood-draw tube is designed to produce a final concentration of *five parts per thousand*. Therefore, a finding of 2 parts per million is the equivalent of zero. Imagine if I were to ask the coroner "Sir, did your extra-fancy detector detect an intruder in the shadows?' Then he might answer 'Why yes, I did.' My next question; 'At this point can you tell the Jury exactly how tall that intruder was?' Then he would have to answer, "Our best estimate is that the intruder was about a tenth of an inch tall.' *Okay, that is not a human being!* Put it another way. When you get into your car and when you've put the key in the ignition, but you haven't turned it yet, you might happen to look down to the speedometer. If you do, and you see the needle just a little below zero, what do you think? Do you think 'Oh my God, I must be going backwards! I sure hope I don't hit something?' Of course not. What you think, if you take any notice of it at all is 'That's just a little variation in where the needle comes to rest when it's not doing anything.' "

The Sergeant-at-Arms called out "Hey, somebody get this guy a soap box."

The Physiologist answered "See me after class, Mr. Powers. You're headed for detention."

"I got news for you, pal. We're all in detention."

"Maybe I got a little off track, but there's a purpose here. My dream was about my own struggles with EDTA. This dream is just a recounting of something really happened. Just before I joined the lab where I did my training, they had reported a finding in the scientific literature. The title was something like this 'Calcium Ions Are Required for Desensitization of Beta-Adrenergic Receptors.' What that means is the following. Beta-receptors are receptors on cells within the body that bind adrenaline and start the response to adrenaline. We isolated one type of white blood cell, lymphocytes, from blood, often drawn from volunteers in the lab, from ourselves. When those lymphocytes, those white blood cells, are exposed to a high concentration of an adrenaline-like drug for an hour or more, desensitization occurs. Desensitization means that you are have lost most of the response to adrenaline. So, in the reported experiment, they threw EDTA into the solution containing the cells and the adrenaline and found that the desensitization did not occur. Desensitization occurred without EDTA, and did not occur when it was added. Since EDTA removes calcium ions from solution, so the interpretation was that calcium ions are needed for desensitization. Wrong. As an incoming grad student, I did a simple test called a trypan blue exclusion test on the cells treated with EDTA and found that they were all dead. So, the finding was invalid. Of course, those cells could not desensitize; that is a function of a living cell."

Claudia "How did you feel about this incident? How does that come out in a dream that you think is interesting enough to share with this group?"

"I'm glad you asked. Actually, this dream was about stress, not problem-solving. My findings were not well-received by the head of the lab and a bit later he told me that he was not happy with my performance, as I had called into question, previous findings from the lab. Here's what I had to do to convince him. I checked the pH of the solution of cells, in other words how acidic that solution is. I checked it just before and just after adding the EDTA. Before EDTA, the cell solution was a neutral, neither acidic or basic and that is the environment in which living things and living cells are happy and healthy. After adding EDTA, the same solution became acidic, almost as much so as stomach contents. And get this: I even supplied the right way to do the experiment. If you want to chelate the calcium ions, if you want to remove them from the solution, you should add not EDTA. Instead you should add *sodium* EDTA to the solution of white blood cells. When EDTA binds calcium, it gives up a hydrogen ion, and that hydrogen ion is what makes the solution acidic and what kills the cells. But when sodium EDTA binds calcium, it gives up a sodium ion, which is harmless. Finally, that is what it took to make the experiment work in a way that was valid. And here's the part that gets to me, even to this day. Solving the problem never got me respected, just begrudgingly tolerated. The overall mood of the dream was stressful. I was being closely watched after making a claim that I had better be able to back up."

The Physiologist went on. "Anyway, as the next dreams starts, I'm climbing out of a swimming pool and begin to walk across the desert. Desert gives way to oak forest and I reach the medical center where I trained, same as above. I scale the brick façade using just my fingers; open a frosted window and climb into the old lab in the Pharmacology Department, a place I revisit from time to time in dreams. Soon, I'm showing off a little trick I devised for keeping white blood cells alive. To isolate the white cells, blood is layered over a syrupy solution called Ficoll-Hypaque and centrifuged. The red cells form sugary clusters and plummet to the bottom, leaving the white cells at the interface between the plasma and the Ficoll. Carefully, that interface is drawn off and then diluted with physiological buffer before recentrifugation, which brings the white cells to the bottom. Here's the bad thing that can happen.

Ficoll is hypertonic, that is, it draws water out of the cells and makes them shrivel. When you dilute with physiological buffer, normalcy is re-established and water re-enters the cell. But if that happens too fast, there can be overshoot. Too much water can enter the cell and the cell will burst. So, here's what I did. I diluted with just a very small amount of physiological buffer, wait one minute, add just a little more and so on, diluting over the course of 10 minutes instead of all at once. That makes all the difference. We get healthy cells, allowing the subsequent experiment to work. I did that same trypan blue test that I described before and instead of getting half the cells alive and half dead as I did with the old method, now all of the cells are alive. And our experiments start working for the first time. I'm talking to a kid who works in the lab; he's got long hair and he looks like he's got some American Indian in him. When I go into the men's room and look at myself, I realize that I too have Indian blood. We take a city bus to his apartment. Out the back window I see a trail leading into the woods. He says, "Out there are forty-one acres in the heart of the city, but developers will never find it." We take that trail and are soon confronted by fifty-foot sheer wall covered with a thick carpet of vines. We climb it with great difficulty, falling many times. In places, I can see the dark red stone that the vines are growing on. At the top, a vista of wild land is spread before us; forest, deer, the sound of running water. I realize my father lives somewhere in there and I can picture him in his war bonnet of turkey feathers.

"Two more, quick if you've got the time." A listless and sleepy crowd looked at him, but there were no objections, so the Physiologist went on. "All up and down the corridor, all fifteen hundred feet of it, yes it really was that long, the whole Pharmacology Department is buzzing about our upcoming visit from the Pope. I have been assigned the role of transporting him from one department to another. We're all doing filter pot experiments and Natasha is frustrated because her data has too much variability. Looking under a microscope, I notice that only one white blood cell is trapped on each filter and that some cells are large and some small. That could be the source of the variation. She asks me to ask the Pope about it when I am transporting him. Take the Pope down a special elevator to a level below the building that is crisscrossed with canals, like Venice. An Italian post-doc is waiting in a motor boat and he knows the way to the next destination. While he pilots the boat,

I run another filter pot experiment on deck. Going up another elevator to the Physiology department, I pose my question to the Pope. He says, 'I'm no expert in this area, but if it were me, I'd make every effort to find out if someone else has already solved the problem.' That sounds like good advice. I realize that person is me. Back at the lab, I normalize Natasha's data to cell size and obtain clean data.

"Now, the last dream. I'm talking to Dan, a fellow grad student who organizes the Department Seminar, same Department, Pharmacology. Dan has extended an invitation to a Peter Gynt, who he says is a famous Norwegian physiologist, although no one else is too sure who he is. Because of the publicity and the large crowd anticipated, Gynt's lecture will be held in an old stone church, the same one where Manitas de Plata recorded his masterpieces of flamenco guitar. As Gynt addresses the audience, he makes an impressive figure, tall, maybe six-five, elderly and with a commanding voice. He spends a short time discussing his own experiments and a long time expounding his theories. Afterwards, there is a reception in the church kitchen; pickles and little white sandwiches with the crusts cut off. Gynt has made a huge impression. Everyone is talking about his theories. Dan tells me later that he is in fact Peter Gynt. I gave him a blank stare because, among other discrepancies, Dan stands only about five-nine and Gynt appeared to be exceptionally tall. "He walks on extra feet" he tells me in his crustiest Norwegian accent and shows me the pair of short stilts that he had kept hidden under baggy pants. Then Dan tells me his motivation. 'I'm sick of no one listening to my theories. I wondered how they would react if they thought those same theories came from a figure of authority. And look, it worked.'

"Dan sounds a lot like you in the first dream." Said the Psychologist."

"Dan is me.

How the Government Set to Work

The rescue operation at Mount Lasser was moving slowly. The only road in and out was covered in thirty feet of snow. There were a great number of officials on the scene, first responders and police. Excavation was still going on the slopes. Dogs were used to sniff out those who remained buried. Such operations are not very hopeful. One hundred ninety were dug up on the slopes and grounds and of those, but only seven alive. The buried skiers were transported by sled, snowmobile or helicopter down the mountain where ambulances waited to take them to hospitals in the area. One hundred and ninety were buried, mostly night skiers and a few who were walking the grounds. Among those, only seven survived. They were easily identified. Most were carrying identification.

Saturday night, the FBI arrived and took charge of operations. It was not until Sunday, the second morning after the attack on Mount Lasser, that a full accounting of the casualties could be made. Two members of the ski patrol were shot and killed while working high above the top of the chair lift. One hundred and forty remained alive at The Tubes, including patrons and employees. One was found shot and dead in a stairwell. That left the nineteen hostages, each of whom were known to someone remaining at The Tubes. Within days, a dossier was compiled for each. Families were notified, but were also warned to report any contact from terrorists and above all, to pay no ransom. The total: one hundred eighty-six dead and nineteen hostages.

Wiring left behind on the mountaintop indicated that the terrorists had used hundreds of sticks of TNT. No wonder it was the biggest avalanche ever seen in California. Surveillance footage from the roof of The Tubes showed that the terrorists had taken away their hostages in a 1978 Sikorsky S-61N utility helicopter, a model which has long since been retired from use by the US military. The S-61N is designed to carry nineteen, including crew. Since the passengers included not only the nineteen hostages, but also an unknown number of terrorists, the craft would have been considerably over-loaded.

The investigation moved quickly and by Monday, the third day after the attack, the Sikorsky transport helicopter was found abandoned in a remote area of the Mendocino National Forest. It would have been a fairly short, but crowded and somewhat dangerous trip. The chopper was left well above the redwoods in an open and flat area that was part grassy meadow and part hard pan. Also abandoned at the site was a small bulldozer which appeared to have been used to level the ground so a plane could take off. Nearby was a stand of Douglas firs that would have made a good place to hide an aircraft or two. The only theory that made sense was that the hostages had been taken from the Mendocino National Forest by jet to a remote location that afforded their captors safe ground.

Both the helicopter and jet could have been purchased legally in the US through a number of legitimate dealers. The helicopter was worth about three million and the jet would have cost a lot more. So, a considerable outlay was made by the terrorists, although they presumably would continue to have use of the jet. The sale of the helicopter was traced using the vehicle's identifying N-number. However, it took the FBI a week to penetrate several layers of deception and learn the true identity of the purchaser. The latter turned out to be Supian Kadiev, a Chechnyan national who was already known to them. Kadiev had purchased both the helicopter and a Gulfstream C-37A jet that holds twelve passengers and five crew and has a range if 6,300 miles. Authorities were disappointed to learn the great range of the jet, which would only increase the difficulty of finding the hostages. What they didn't know is that the seats had been removed and an extra fuel tank installed and as result, the range of the jet was even greater. Kadiev had fled the country in the days prior to the attack. Although no computers belonging to him were recovered, he was known to have ties to separatist movements both in Chechnya and Indonesia.

The dossier for the Navy Pilot included a most fortunate detail, namely that he had tracking device implanted in his calf. He had requested it because, on retirement from the Navy, he had planned to climb mountains in some very remote regions. It was estimated that the signal put out by the tracking device could be detected by reconnaissance aircraft at a maximum distance of one hundred miles. The device was recharged by the motion of his leg in walking. Air surveillance of Chechnya was good enough to be sure that the terrorists were not there. Despite the troubling fact that points in Indonesia are as much as 8,600 miles from Northern California, a decision was made to begin a grid search of the island nation. It would be a daunting task considering that they were dealing with two thousand islands spread across two thousand miles of ocean.

At this point, the identity and the aims of the terrorists were still a mystery. Among radical organizations hostile to the US and the West in general, none claimed responsibility. Several released statements specifically denying responsibility, of course without expressing that they were in any way unhappy with the results.

The Sergeant-at-Arms' Tale

The fifth morning found the group again quiet at breakfast. It was not for lack of interest in the food. They had rice and beans and cups of water that tasted of sulfur. There was also a bowl of uncooked peanuts. Silence blanketed the group like a jungle fog. The showing of scars and telling of dreams had each run its course. For a short while, a rooster began to crow in the in the yard in front of the compound and then stopped. Across the morning gloom, the Physiologist proposed a new idea to all. "Have you ever read the Canterbury Tales by Chaucer? It's about a group of pilgrims were traveling to a shrine in Canterbury. Each evening at an inn, they would amuse each other by telling stories. We could do the same. I think it would be fun."

This idea struck a chord with the Sergeant-at-Arms and he immediately volunteered to be the first. His arm shot up in the air. "Teacher, teacher. Pick me. Pick me." There were no objections among the listless group, and so the Sergeant-at-Arms began.

"Good morning ladies and gentlemen. I'm Arnie Powers and I'm so god-damned proud to be here today. Don't this just look like the fur on a polar bear [rubbing his hand over his thick and pure white crew cut]? I've been this way since I was thirty. I'm fifty-four years old right now, not that you care. But at thirty, I was still the main muscle for the Knuckle Draggers. I was their Sergeant-at-Arms. Today I'm just the President. That's just a job for an old guy.

Let me begin by saying that I've probably made enough crank to keep the entire West coast of the United States awake through a week-long public television pledge drive. And if you believe that to be possible, then more power to ye. I'll tell you what though, just about everyone is on it, crank that is. Ma'am [eyeing at Mrs. White] I know you've tried it. Disapproving of everything in sight take a lot of energy.

Besides, everyone has been on crank at one time or another; even Santa and his reindeer. How do you think they're able to fly through the sky like that and do it the whole night of Christmas Eve? How do you think they visit millions of homes in just one night? Did you think that was just snow on their noses? Hell, I make a product that does not need advertising. It is literally the glue that holds our great nation together and best of all, it's made right here in the US of fuckin A. Alright, now, on to my story."

Mrs. White stood in front of the Sergeant-at-Arms with her hands firmly on her hips "Disgusting." She pronounced.

"Hey, everyone. I just received a request to clean up my language. Dear Church Lady, I take pen in hand to address your concerns. Please be assured that, in accordance with all the known principles of customer service, your request has been heard......carefully considered......*and* rejected. If you want to control the way a story is told, then I suggest you tell your own story. For my own part, I maintain my first amendment rights. You do believe in the Constitution, don't you? I maintain the right to express myself in my own way. You see, folks, I'm the same Great White everywhere I go. I'm not a chameleon, like some people. Now on to the story.

"Once upon a time, boys and girls, in a faraway land, I guess that's the way a fairy tale ought to begin, though I'm not so sure about the part where everyone lives happily ever after. Anyway, once upon a time, there was a man who lived in a great tower made of green glass. Now, the green glass of that tower was manufactured in a special kind of way, so that from his big corner office, he could see out, but you couldn't see in. Or at least that's what he liked to tell himself. But in fact, any fool with twenty-twenty vision could easily see the small man behind the curtain.

"The man in the tower was an Executive, that's spelled with a capital E and he had what we call narcissistic personality disorder. The executive, whose name was Robert, had a head so damned big that he could barely get through the door to the boardroom. I don't think I'm too far out of line to say that his condition is quite common among the most successful of his peers, and he was nothing if not a successful man. He had a horde of underlings who reported to him, directly or indirectly, and many of them were professionals in their own right. He spent a lot of time attending to his own importance, which needed to be cataloged and recorded, announced and broadcast on a constant basis in order to keep him sufficiently occupied to prevent him from dwelling on his insecurities, and the man was riddled with insecurities.

He had assembled his Yuppie profile in a way that was sorely lacking in imagination. Mercedes? Check. Armani suits? Check. Private jet? Check. Collect expensive wines? Check. Tooth whitening? You bet, after his wife started addressing him as 'Skeletor'. You remember Skeletor from He-Man and the Masters of the Universe. One morning, the Executive found a sign taped to his office door. It read 'Stress? I don't get stress; I give stress!' Upon reading it, a big broad smile had spread across the Executive's face. Whoever put the sign there might have imagined it would embarrass him, but no. He saw it as validation.

"I like to see you try to make it in business." called out the Executive.

"I have, bro. I'm worth over 50 mil. If I had my cell phone, I'd show you a picture of my house; ten bedrooms, dirt track, soundstage, bar, big pool with an oasis of palm trees for our parties. And get this; right in front of the house is an eighteen-foot tall concrete gorilla with his knuckles dragging in the dirt. The property used to be a mini-golf and I kept that part.

"Dude has some attitude." the Second Engineer was overheard saying.

The Sergeant-at-Arms continued. "Thank you, and now let's get back to this Executive, the one *he* [eying the Executive] is trying to stop me from talking about. But I want you to know this; word *will* get out. The Great White will see to that. Now, Robert, the hero of our story, he spoke a dialect of the English language that I like to refer to as Nipper, because it's basically what you hear when you turn on National Public Radio."

"I happen to like NPR. I listen to it on our local public radio station every day." objected Lauren Campbell.

"Now don't get me wrong; I sometimes listen to it myself. And I admit that NPR is a good source of information, but I have to turn down the volume when they start talking Nipper. Actually, they have two ways of talking that get to me. One is that delicate whispering that broadcasts 'I care' in capital letters. Virtue signaling at its worst. I mean, get off it, people. Life deals a lot of hard blows, and we need to talk about them in a *forthright* manner. In doing so, we show that we understand and accept the world as it is. It's not about you; it's not about your feelings. The world is fully prepared to move forward without each and every one of us. And don't try to paint me as some kind of redneck. What I'm saying is exactly the same as the advice you might get from your friendly neighborhood Zen master. The other way they have of talking, the one that really gets me, is Nipper. Nipper is marked by a special kind of manufactured imperturbability. At all costs, let's not get excited. Forget about defending yourself and just pretend you are not threatened, even if you are. Picture a typical NPR reporter, and now imagine that he has been sentenced to death by lethal injection. His response to the judge, in Nipper of course, might go something like this. 'Well, a host of observations immediately spring to mind. One, this is indeed bad news; but not so bad, nor nearly so painful, as that host of privations visited upon our ancestors by their violent enemies. To wit: the Vikings practiced a form of ritual torture and murder known as the bloody eagle....' Nippers seem to believe that when challenged or insulted, the best thing to do is show that you are not concerned. That's metrosexual-speak. And by the way, can we get rid of words like hipster and metrosexual and just go back to calling it pussy?

It's true, you shouldn't let yourself be undone by every little thing, but here's where they get it wrong. Let's take the example of a boxer. True, he shouldn't, as they say, get into a fight on the way to the arena. But let's get one thing straight; it's what you do once you get to the arena that counts. My question to all the Nippers of this world is this. It's all well and good to say on a given occasion 'this is not my arena', but in the end, I still have to ask, 'where *is* your arena?' How do we defend ourselves when we are legitimately challenged? That is one big test of our worth and character. Seems to me like you're doing everything you can to avoid that test, Mr. Nipper Man.

Anyway, back to the Robert and *his* important story. As we begin, he has just received some bad news from his doctor. A week earlier, he had experienced an episode of chest pain. He had become dizzy and just generally felt like shit to the point where he checked himself into the ER. A blood test now revealed that he had actually suffered a small heart attack, a warning sign to be sure. He resolved to do everything in his power to protect his health. After all, what could be more important than his own well-being? And he was still a young man. It was obvious that first and foremost, he would have to give up smoking and he discussed this at length with his wife. He had tried cold turkey in the past. He tried the patch. He tried Chantix. He even tried those little cigarette holders where you dial down the smoke. He had tried everything you can imagine. His wife suggested a hypnotist.

Now Robert's wife was quite a piece of work herself; a former model and a stunning five-foot nine-inch natural red head with a rack that wouldn't quit. She was followed by a pack of howling wolves everywhere she went. She never wore high heels; Robert wouldn't allow that. Even without heels, she was two inches taller. The wife was also a genuinely insincere person. And that is just so rare to find these days. So why wouldn't she cheat on Robert? In fact, she was currently cheating with the very same hypnotist whose services she had just suggested. I should also add that the wife felt very self-righteous about her infidelities because she happened to know about a woman that the Executive was currently seeing. She suggested a hypnotist by the name of Jeremy.

'Who is this guy, baby?' Robert asked.

'Oh, he's really famous.' she said. And by that she meant famous for nine inches, which is what she had heard from her friend Natalie and then just had to find out for herself. Now isn't *that* nice? 'Jeremy is not cheap' she added, 'but he has helped Natalie. He straightened out her insides.' And here, she couldn't help laughing a little to herself.

Mrs. White looked a little puzzled. She certainly would have been outraged by this last little bit, had she understood it. But that mortar sailed straight over her head.

'Huh?' said Robert to his wife; he was a little skeptical.

'That's psych talk, babe.' she informed him. 'Natalie got herself satisfied psychologically, on the inside, you know.'

'What the hell has that got to do with me?' he shot back. Robert was now was irritated, as intended.

'Honey, Jeremy has helped so many people quit smoking. I'm

surprised you haven't heard about it.'

'Actually, I've heard that hypnotism doesn't work all that well.'

She said 'That all depends on which hypnotist you are talking about. Jeremy is really a big hypnotherapist and he has a nearly one hundred percent success rate. Hypnotism isn't like taking a pill, you know. You are actually the one who does it, you are the one who quits smoking. But in order for Jeremy to help you, first he needs to gain your trust. Trust is the whole issue. Jeremy is very good at gaining people's trust. He's good at *earning* their trust. That's what makes him a star.'

And so, after a while, the Robert set aside the small voice that told him something wasn't exactly right. He agreed to go see the hypnotist. His wife accompanied him on his first visit. Throughout the first stages of the session, the wife and Jeremy kept very straight faces and stuck close to the script. Knowing glances were exchanged between them. Jeremy started by getting Robert under a trance. Later, he would describe the Robert as extremely easy to hypnotize. He went so far as to say that he was the most gullible person he had worked with yet. Jeremy made suggestions along two lines. First were all the standard suggestions that Robert would find cigarettes and the smell of smoke disgusting. Second, he would always want his wife to be present at the sessions. As always, he was told that he would not remember any of the suggestions he had received. After one session, he was already smoking less and was well pleased."

The Executive called out again "Are you quite finished? Because when you are, I have a story.'

The Sergeant-at-Arms replied. "Finished? Hell no! This was just the first session. In the next session, our two heroes decided to have even a little more fun at Robert's expense. Where was the harm, after all? He wouldn't even remember what had happened while he was under. So, after the usual suggestions about not smoking, Jeremy leaned in a little too close and asked a seemingly sympathetic question.

'Robert, do you like bananas?'

'Do I like bananas? Sure, I like bananas.'

'Good. Robert, I'm going to peel a banana for you and I want you to eat it. This banana is going to be the most delicious thing you have ever eaten.'

Robert finished the banana and he was grinning from ear to ear. 'Wow' he exclaimed without being prompted. 'I never knew a banana could taste like that.'

'That's very good, Robert. You are doing well.' said Jeremy in his most syrupy voice. 'And now, Robert, I'm going to show you another banana and this time I want you to imagine that this banana belongs to a very important man. Robert, this man is important because there is a very big deal on the line. This is a situation that means a lot to you. You can make a great deal of money here. Can you imagine that for me?' The wife giggled and Jeremy put a finger to his lips.

'Yes, Jeremy. I can do that.'

'Now Robert, I want you to know beforehand that whatever goes on between you and this man stays entirely between the two of you. No one else will ever know.'

'It's a secret. I get that.'

'Robert, this man is now going to feed you his banana. Only this time, it will be a banana that has not been peeled. And also, and this is important; I want you to really take your time and enjoy it. Enjoy it even more than you did even the last banana. Robert, I want you to close your eyes.'

'OK, I'm ready.' Robert beamed back at him. And with that, Jeremy slowly introduced the tip of the banana into the Executive's mouth."

"Alright, that's enough. I've had it. This is simply beyond the limit of decency." intoned Mrs. White, again with her hands on her hips.

"Ma'am, I'm gonna have to ask you to get over that Church Lady thing you've got going on. This story has an important moral lesson, especially for the younger people in the audience. And your interruptions make it harder for me to get to that lesson across, harder for me to make that point."

"I think you *and* your characters are disgusting, immoral individuals." And with that, she stalked away to another part of the room and did not hear the rest of the story.

The Sergeant-at-Arms now addressed the rest of the group.

"Actually, I never said they were nice people. And doesn't she know there are bad people even in the Bible? Anyway, it's probably a good thing that she left. I don't think she's ready to hear what happened next. You see, this incident with the banana, well the wife had recorded the whole thing on her cell phone and she and Jeremy replayed over and over it during their trysts. They would act out the scene together. And she would say little nothings to him like 'Oh Jeremy, you are such an important man. I need your banana in my mouth right now.' And then they would roll around laughing, so much so that they were almost unable to have sexual intercourse. Almost, I said.

"But after a while, the newness of their little joke began to wear off and they both knew they needed come up with something extra. At the next hypnotherapy session, she even let Jeremy jump her bones right in front of her husband. They even asked him to film it on her phone and he did so willingly. Jeremy told Robert in the most serious voice he could muster 'Robert, you are my star reporter, the number one ace on this newspaper staff. An important current event is about to take place and I'm trusting you to film it using this phone. Can you do that for me, Robert?' And, as you might expect, because Jeremy was good at what he did, Robert complied fully and after the trance was broken, he didn't remember a thing. Once Robert was out of his trance, the conversation turned serious and Jeremy said, 'I'm very pleased with the *thrust* of tonight's session.'

"Now you really *are* finished. My turn." called out the Executive.

"Finished, except to say this. I think I was wrong when I said I wasn't so sure about the part where everyone lives happily ever after. Turns out that everyone did *get* what they wanted in the end. Robert really did quit smoking and for good. Whatever you do to improve your health; why that has to be a good thing! The wife and Jeremey had their fun and no one was the wiser. So, I have to say, it's a nice, uplifting little story, all in all. And with that, I say it really *is* your turn now. Have at it, bro."

The Executive's Tale

The Executive was chomping at the bit and it seemed only fair that he should go next. If he was undone by all barbs he had received from the Sergeant-at-Arms, it didn't show. In fact, he looked relaxed as he stood with one hand leaning against the chair where his suit jacket lay folded.

"We all know each other by now, but just to repeat, I'm Martin Pelli. As I've mentioned before, I'm majority stockholder and CEO of Lansing Nutraceuticals. No doubt you've seen our products in health stores and supermarkets. Despite the name Lansing, we're based out of Los Angeles and today I'm going to tell you an L.A. story. This is the story of Donna Marrero. The story as a whole is more or less true. Most of it is literally true and has been published in the L.A. Times. All I've done is fill in a few small details just to make the story flow. So, I don't expect to encounter a lot of objections because, as I said. the story is basically true. Correction: I actually *do* expect objections; I just don't expect to take them seriously *or* not to enjoy them.

"Now Donna Marrero is, or was, a well-known lawyer, activist and philanthropist in the Mexican-American community. I used to see her on TV when there were fund-raisers and similar events. She was always wearing a blue and yellow scarf that hung down past her waist. That was a trademark and she did it to help people recognize her. She was a lady of a certain age who never seemed to age further over the many years that I saw her.

"From accounts in the newspaper, published mostly after her fall from grace, I've gleaned a little of the life history of Donna Marrero. She was a housewife well into her thirties. Then her husband, the owner of a Chevy dealership, died unexpectedly. After that, her fortunes improved dramatically and somewhat surprisingly. The husband had had no known health problems and the cause of death was never determined because Donna had moved quickly to have the body cremated. She got the dealership, which she sold, and the insurance money.

"She had always harbored a deep desire to be an assertive and important person and like many in her position, it occurred to her that law school might be the shortest route to that end. In fact, she had just finished law school at the time of her husband's death. In the next year, she and a partner founded Marrero and Moore and they quickly gained publicity as woman-owned business. Mostly, they represented Chicanos in discrimination and visa cases. They were closely aligned with the Mexican American Legal Defense Fund. The firm seemed to be thriving and Donna began to donate her services to local causes. Notably, she raised money for scholarships. The publicity served her well and she gained a reputation as a socialite and philanthropist, but I think her contribution to the community was more in time than money. I don't think she was really all that wealthy, or in the end, generous.

"What first made me doubt her wealth was reading about her opening a boarding house for older men. That struck me as maybe providing a decent income, but not a way to get rich. It was presented as a public service, but I wondered. The house was in Echo Park on Douglas near the 101 freeway and not far from Dodger Stadium. The tenants were of all backgrounds, not just Latino. Donna's running of the boarding house was seen as an act of charity, with the result that her reputation was enhanced. Many of the residents were no longer mentally competent or had become so during their stay. Eventually most signed over power of attorney over to Donna and their monthly Social Security checks were deposited directly into her account. It was eventually learned that Donna received checks each month far in excess of the actual number of residents living in her building.

The Lawyer was first to object. "Yo! Flaco [skinny]! This story better not be about me because, if it is, I'm gonna sue your ass as soon as we get back home. I'm not a public figure and you have no protection against libel."

"Nice, very nice. Only Donna Marrero is *not* you. She is a real person. Not only that, but I think you've heard of her. You're from California and this was a big story. It broke around 2005. I'm dead certain that you've read about her."

The Lawyer turned her head just a little and said nothing. It was clear that she now realized that she had heard of Donna Marrero after all. And with that, the Executive continued, infused with new energy. "The boarding house in question was a rambling Victorian. At one time, it had been a public grade school and when it closed, Donna had been able to buy it from the county for a song, due to her connections. The house had had considerable grounds, more than any other house in the neighborhood. She had a handy man and gardener named Arnie. This Arnie was a little slow on the uptake and he admired Donna Marrero as if she were a queen."

"Bullshit. His name was Hector or something like that." said Arnie, the Sergeant-at-Arms, that is.

"His name was Arnie. You can look it up."

"You say that only because you know damn well we can't look it up. I say his name was Hector."

"Excellent. Excellent. Thank you for your interest in the character. I'm sorry that you identify with him. Now, let me go on to describe Arnie a little better. He was short and his deck was even shorter. Arnie inhabited a mysterious grey zone that exists in the realm of human sympathy. Let me explain. I've noticed that we have a curious way of looking at people of limited mental capacity. We tend to look down on them and the dumber they are, the more we do so. However, when a person's mental capacity is low enough to be described as outright disabled, then at this point, we do an abrupt about-face and the person becomes instead, a figure of sympathy. Making fun of a stupid person is socially acceptable. Making fun of the retarded, or whatever term you prefer; that is clearly not. So, as I was saying, Arnie inhabited the grey zone between the two categories and as a result, he was treated by some with contempt and by others with sympathy.

"I bet I have a higher IQ than you do, dude." said the Sergeant-at-Arms. "One forty-six; that's Mensa-grade. Can you beat that? Can you?"

"Thank you. Your indignation is greatly appreciated. Now let me go on to say that it wasn't hard at all for Donna Marrero to wrap the little man around her little finger. She had a lot of tools to do that. She could be imperious, cold and demanding. Most of the time, Arnie was scared to death of her. But she also knew that we catch more flies with honey. And so, from time to time, she would kiss him on the cheek or forehead and call him her Papi Chulo. Such a gesture could fuel his imagination for weeks and months. He felt almost like a husband, serving and protecting her. Papi Chulo; it was their little secret.

There was a garage in a corner of the property. Arnie had a bed in there and the rest of the space was for tools and equipment needed to maintain the building and grounds. She had bought him a work bench and tools for carpentry and plumbing. There was a riding mover, leaf blower, chainsaw and hedge trimmer. Mysteriously, she had also bought Arnie a backhoe. She said it was for occasional landscaping jobs, but really that didn't seem to make sense.

It was assumed she made a good living from her law practice. And she had a steady income from the boarding house. But her finances were not as they seemed. Donna had expensive tastes and she had made mistakes in investing. In fact, she was drowning in debt. Finally, she hit upon a solution. She realized that once she gained power of attorney for one of her residents, the man himself was no longer needed and she could continue to collect his monthly pension, social security, and disability checks forever. Right after her epiphany, that's when Arnie got his backhoe.

One fateful morning, Donna called Arnie into her office for a very important job. But before I tell you about that job, I have to back up and tell you how Donna did something crafty to ensure both that Arnie would accept his new assignment and that he would be up it. Donna started by breaking from protocol and inviting Arnie to a home-cooked dinner in her private quarters. He had only been there once or twice before and never for a meal. The mood he walked into was intimate. The lights were off and only candles lit the dining room. She served what she had learned was a favorite meal that his mother had made, chicken mole with yuccas and nopalitoes on the side. That last one is slices of cactus cooked together with onion, tomato and tomatillo. I love it myself. Over dinner, she got Arnie tipsy on red wine. Suffice it to say that the evening progressed as planned and Arnie spent the night in Donna's bed. No one will ever know if the arrangement was consummated in the literal sense because who could be sure of Arnie's ability to act the part of a man? And Donna certainly isn't telling. I imagine she had had to swallow a good deal of pride to go through with her plan, but it was for a sound purpose and so in the end, she did. Donna was only about forty-five at the time and still a looker. So, it was a hell of a come down for her. But the incident was burned deeply into Arnie's consciousness and in the next days, recalling it accounted for 99% of his total brain activity."

At this point, The Executive stopped for a sip of water and shot a look toward the Sergeant-at-Arms, who was looking bored and fidgety. There was no response, so the Executive continued. "Fast-forward one week and Donna is now calling Arnie into her office. 'Papi Chulo, I have an important job for you.' She was whispering. 'I need you to be very diligent today. I need you to be the very best you can. Can you do that for me?' On hearing this, Arnie stood just a little taller. She took him into the basement and showed him a bundle, wrapped in an old rug and tied up tightly in heavy twine. She said 'Papi, this is something very important that I want you to bury on the property. I'll show you exactly where.' The purpose of the backhoe was now apparent. They went outside and she showed him where to dig. 'I want you to dig a hole that is very, very deep; six feet deep. When you stand inside the hole, the ground will be over your head. Do you understand? Dig the hole and when you are finished, come find me. I want to see it before you put the rug inside. And here is the most important part. Do not look inside the carpet. Do not look inside under any circumstances. Do you understand me?' She kissed Arnie on the cheek and left him to his digging.

Arnie never asked any questions, but one can easily imagine what was going on in his mind, or more precisely, what wasn't. We've all sat at a table where people are eating and there is a dog begging, waiting patiently for any scraps that may come his way. So, what does the dog think? Does it think 'How unfair! People eat whenever they want, but I get fed if and when they think it's OK.'? Of course not. Dogs aren't capable of that kind of thought. They just blankly accept things at face value. Well, that's how I think it was with Arnie. He just dug the hole, that's all. He already knew how to use the backhoe, as Donna had given him a couple of small landscaping jobs. When he had the hole deep and wide enough for Donna Marrero's satisfaction, Arnie drove the backhoe in through the double doors of the basement and picked up the bundle. Then he buried it and covered the hole and that was the end of it.

The first victim was named Alan Cooper and immediately his monthly checks became much more valuable with no room and board to deduct. Quickly, Donna rented his room to another man. For the next victim, she thought to have the hole dug in advance. That way she minimized her window of exposure. The plan worked marvelously well for a while. No one missed these men. She was careful to choose the ones with no family. At a boarding house, this is usually the case for most. Over the next years, one man after another was buried on the grounds and slowly Donna Marrero got out of debt. She even became comfortable again. She expanded her role in the community and began spending money again, buying a new Lincoln and taking trips to Mexico and Europe.

Then one day, things began to go terribly wrong. The house of cards began to fall and there was no way to put it back up. The newspaper did not tell exactly how the police got on to Donna Marrero, but it isn't hard to imagine. Although Donna had been careful, neighbors could have witnessed some of the digging and there would have been talk. An IRS agent did come looking for a resident who turned out to be long dead. Among other things, he might have noticed a fresh grave site with no grass growing over it. Also, I think she may have underestimated the curiosity of her residents. Thirteen so-called heart attacks is a lot. And never once did they see a hearse come to take a body away. So, one of them might have easily called the police.

In any case, the Sherriff's Department did arrive and began digging up the yard. The digging took a week and was quite a scene. The property was sealed off, with reporters and gawkers crowding the perimeter. Updates could be seen every evening on KTLA News. Dolores, this is the part you saw at the time." The Executive looked over at the Lawyer, who felt compelled to give up just a fraction of a smile.

The Executive went on. "A total of thirteen bodies were recovered from the grounds, all wrapped in rugs or blankets. Forensic testing yielded indirect evidence of cyanide poisoning. The L.A. Times report said cyanide itself lasts only a day or two in a dead body, but its metabolites persist in the liver and bones of the deceased. The use of cyanide made sense. Cyanide is a fast-acting poison and Donna would have wanted her victims to disappear quickly without a prolonged illness that could have aroused suspicion in the other residents. From there, things devolved quickly. Arnie told his story. Faced with a mountain of evidence, Donna confessed. After a very public sentencing, she moved to her new home at the California Institute for Women in Chino. Arnie was never charged.

"And so, ends a heart-warming story. Is there a moral? Not really. No one needs to be reminded not to be like out two heroes. But I would like to end with a brief comparison between myself and my friend Mr. Arnie Powers. He engages in unprovoked attacks. I do not. He makes a product that destroys lives. My products improve life. Now, concerning his theories about Nippers and their manufactured imperturbability…. I propose the following. Imperturbability is not a dodge, not an avoidance of any test. Instead, it represents self-control. In life, the cool-headed prevail, just as I hope you will agree that I have just done in this opening round."

And with that, the Executive received a smattering of applause from several of his listeners.

What the Physiologist Heard

Having listened to these two tales, told by the Sergeant-at-Arms and the Executive, the Physiologist was tired and he went back to bed. He had received some chemo just a few months earlier and he still often slept during the day. There was a second motive for his going back to bed. He had noticed that two among them, Hi and Sunny, were spending a lot of time together, off by themselves. Hi and Sunny were off in a corner talking. The Physiologist's bed was close enough to them that he could pretend to sleep, while having a chance to eavesdrop. It looked like something was happening between the two.

The Physiologist pulled the blanket up over his head and soon he was having a dream in which he could not reach his wife, Rene. He saw her in the distance and called to her but she couldn't hear him. She was at the far end of the same park where he had skated as a child. She was ten or twelve years old. He had always wanted to know her as a child. He ran after her and barricades kept being inserted between them. Rows of apartments; he climbed the rooftops with ease. But as he sprang from one rooftop to the next, new roofs were inserted and soon, she disappeared from his sight. He took out his cell phone but, at first, he couldn't remember her number. Finally, he brought it to mind. Then there were problems with the phone, which was an antique piece of military junk weighing five pounds. The buttons for the numbers were too close together; his finger would hit two or three buttons at the same time. He kept having to redial. He would have needed a pencil or pen to push those buttons, but he didn't have one. Then the Physiologist woke up or partly woke up. He realized he couldn't move. Sleep paralysis; he'd had it before; he knew it wouldn't last. He just lay still and let the feeling of the dream slowly drift away. He could hear Hi and Sunny. Here's what he overheard.

"Hi. Sunny. I'm Hi."

"I remember. Hi, Hi."

A brief pause.

"Hi. Is that short for something?"

"Guess."

"Hiram?"

"No."

"Hyman? Like Hyman Roth in the Godfather?"

"No, again."

"Chaim, seriously?"

"None of those."

"Good. Those names are way too old-fashioned, anyway. Hiawatha; that must be it."

"No. It's actually short for High Pressure System. So, you see, Miss Sunny, we're compatible, in a meteorological sorta way. High and Sunny. It's a weather forecast. We can't stop it any more than we can change the weather."

"That's OK, Mr. High Pressure. I get it. You're not proud of your real name, so who am I to judge? Just don't try any of your high-pressure tactics on me. I'm a delicate flower, can't you see?"

"I can see that you've got that whole Olive Oyl thing goin on. That's what I can see."

"By the way, Hi and Sunny might be just a little optimistic as a forecast for us. Dark and stormy is more like it. But anyway, tell me a little about yourself."

"Let's see. My parents started a chain of sushi restaurants. The family has five restaurants, all in Southern California. The one on Melrose Avenue right near Fairfax High is mine. I was named area high school basketball player of the decade by the LA Times. I have the California amateur record for water ski jumping. That's what I do now. I've won contests up and down the coast of Southern California."

"Is that right?"

"Two hundred eighty-two feet to be exact."

"That's maybe a little too exact for me."

"What's the matter?"

"How about this. Why don't you try telling me about something else besides your accomplishments?"

"Such as what?"

"Problems. I'd like to hear about your problems."

"I don't know…"

"Sure, you do. Everybody has problems. Get rid of that armor you wear around."

"I know everyone has problems. I just don't talk about them."

"Well I want to hear them. Come on now, cough it up. If I don't know your problems, I don't really know *you*."

"You really want to hear that kind of thing?"

"I know it's hard for you, but yes, I really *do* want to hear that kind of thing."

"OK, I guess. Just recently, I caught my Dad cheating."

"That's what I'm talking about."

"I was out at a restaurant, way across town, where they probably thought no one would see them. I spotted them in the back and I'm pretty sure they spotted me. She was an old neighbor from when I was growing up in Gardena. My parents live in Brentwood now. I was shocked. I couldn't help asking myself: has this been going on all these years? I asked for the check and left without finishing my meal."

"See? You are human. You have problems, like the rest of us. You're not just a guy who wins awards. What else? Do you have any problems with a girlfriend?"

"I don't have a girlfriend right now. But I suppose that is a problem, or at least the result of a problem."

"Noted." After a moment of silence, Sunny continued. So, let's go on. Do you notice anything missing from the conversation so far?"

"Yes, OK. I haven't asked you about yourself. Is that it?" After another short silence, Hi continued. There was a very ordinary exchange of information between the two about such things as: where have you lived? Do you have siblings? What are your parents like?

Then Sunny changed the subject. "What do you think about that biker and his lawyer?"

"What do you mean?"

"I think there's something going on between them."

"Seriously."

"Do you see the way they touch each other when they think no one is watching? It's a sign of what I call past intimacy. But they have to hide it here, in front of strangers. That's the funny part. It's like they're back in high school, hiding it from Mom and Dad. Seriously, can't you just picture them when they get a moment?"

Hi spoke up first. "Howdy ma'am. You sure are lookin like a grade A side of beef tonight."

"Why, you're just my type." Sunny clasped her hands together and sighed. "I like my men with short legs and a mullet." They both burst out laughing. And soon they were in each other's arms, kissing. The Physiologist could hear it all. He didn't move a muscle.

The two broke apart for a second as Hi protested. "Now wait a second. I've been told I have short legs."

"I'll make an exception for you. For now, that is. But if this relationship is going to last, you're going to have to do something about those legs."

The Heiress's Tale

After the Executive had finished, the Musician noticed a copper-colored rooster by the wall, searching the concrete floor for scraps. Probably the same one who had crowed outside in the yard, he thought. But how did he get inside? The Musician took a peanut from the bowl on the table, shelled it and tossed a half kernel in the direction of the rooster, who snapped it up. The Musician tossed out more peanuts and lured closer the rooster, who obviously was not shy. Finally, it flapped its wings and landed on the table. Then, slowly, the bird began to march the perimeter of the tabletop and as it did, regarded each of the captives, looking them over carefully, both up and down, and giving off an aura as if it thought them all foolish. It seemed to ask: Who are you? What are you doing? Attacking each other, when each other is all you have right now? The bird jumped down from the table and strutted off.

Then Heiress said to no one in particular "I had a dream last night. In the middle of the night, I lay awake, but I wasn't really awake. I was only awake *within* the dream. I was floating, up near the ceiling, and I looked way down to a circle of light around the table lamp below where I saw the tiny little figure of myself trying to put together the pieces of a jigsaw puzzle. She was using a hammer, trying to make the mismatched pieces fit and stamping her feet when it didn't work. I had to laugh at the foolishness. The pieces were half as big as she was and she had to use both hands to move them. She slammed the hammer down on the pieces that wouldn't fit. That's so stupid, I thought. What is she doing? And then, somehow, I was able to send a message down to her, down to the table where she sat below. I told her 'Take those pieces apart and let them sit on the table. And above all, be patient. In the end, they will show you of their own accord, how they are meant to fit together.' So that's my plan going forward and I think it's something we all might consider."

"Amen." said the Physician.

"Nicely put." echoed the Psychologist.

"That's my thought for the moment." The Heiress continued. "Oh, and I have a story, too. It's a different kind of story. I'm Carol Osterberg and some of you may remember me from the old TV ads for Carol's Custard. I was Carol. I am Carol. The story I'm going to tell you is a tragedy that occurred in my family. It's the story of the kidnapping and murder of my Uncle Gil. You see, this is my second encounter with kidnapping. It's a story that will hit home with all of us. I only hope it ends better for us than it did for Gil."

"Sorry to break you chain of thought, but I do remember those ads." said the Psychologist. "We had them in North Carolina. But I don't recognize you at all."

"Well, of course not. I was eight years old and the golden braids - that was a wig. Do you remember how artificially bright it was, like a neon sign? That was the idea, you know, to make it memorable."

"OK, I'm ready! Roll the camera." said the Psychologist. "Say I'm your father Jim and we're sitting at a picnic table beside a Carol's Custard restaurant. When the announcer is done, I turn to the camera and say, 'and now here's Carol with a message for all."

"Yes! And then I say my line, which was 'Enjoy the frozen goodness of whole milk and fresh eggs at Carol's Custard'. That's not exactly Madison Avenue, is it? In fact, it sounds pretty damn corny in the retelling, but a lot of TV was like that back then. And corny fit the Osterbergs hand-in-glove. The spirit of those ads also permeated our lives.

"I was taught to hate ostentation and I still do. Dad and Uncle Gil started as ordinary dairy farmers, but by the time I came along, my family and my cousin's family each had farms with thousands of acres. A few years before I was born, and I'm the youngest of four, my father and my Uncle Gil obtained a bank loan and expanded their business into milk processing and distribution. Osterberg Farms milk and our other dairy products quickly became a familiar sight on the supermarket shelf and went on to become the third largest dairy business in the country. We processed virtually all the milk produced in the southern half of the state, parts of Minnesota and Iowa, too. We still do.

"The year I was born, they opened the first Carol's custard restaurant. I was born into a comfortable home, but during my childhood, we became very wealthy. As I said, I'm the youngest of four. Maryann is the oldest, followed by Jim and Larsen. I'm fourteen years younger than Maryann and I think I'm probably an accident. But accidents can be happy, can't they? Mother was forty when she had me and she developed severe phlebitis in her legs during the pregnancy. So, it is very lucky that we both are here. Here on this earth, I mean. Mother is still alive but far away of course. She's ninety-two. Dad's gone. I can only imagine what she's going through now.

"The Osterbergs had success, but we stayed in the same farm house, one that was only a little more comfortable than those of our neighbors. The house has two stories and a steeply pitched roof. It is white, with board and batten construction, green asphalt shingles on the roof. It has a big porch with the roof supported by square white columns. There was not a single element of decoration on the house. Our cousins were half a mile down the road.

"The Osterbergs had few luxuries and we liked it that way. My parents weren't practicing any kind of restraint. They simply regarded showing off as something that only a fool would do. Our custard stores were plain and there were simple wooden picnic tables outside. We provided a good product at a reasonable price, no frills. We ran the business a little differently than they did at Dairy Twirl. They had franchises and you'd see a variety of names; Doug's Dairy Twirl, Connie's Dairy Twirl. For a long time, my family owned all our stores and when we finally did sell franchises, we kept the name Carol's Custard for all our stores.

"So, back to the story of Uncle Gil. On a crisp morning in October 1975, one of our milk trucks was traveling down a country road, not far from our cousin's house. It was the route that Gil took every morning to his office in the processing plant. My father had taken the same route a little earlier. Both men had fixed habits. The truck driver stopped and sounded his horn because there was a car straddling the white line at an odd angle. The road was narrow and he could not get past the old and beat-up canary-yellow Mercury that was parked in the middle of the road with the driver's side door hanging open, the engine running and the radio playing. An ominous sign, to be sure. While he was waiting for the police to arrive, the driver of the milk truck found a brown fedora by the side of the road. It belonged to Uncle Gil.

"It didn't take long to figure out what had happened. The Mercury was blocking the road, forcing Gil to stop. It was then that the kidnapper must have confronted him. He preferred to drive Gil's car, a late-model green and white Plymouth station wagon. He took it and left his own car behind. Perhaps he did that because the Plymouth was a better car, in better mechanical shape. Maybe his own car ran very poorly and would have made an unreliable getaway vehicle. Anyway, the Mercury led them straight to the kidnapper. Not only that, but the police would also know to look for Gil's vehicle on the highways. Talk about a stupid criminal. He must have turned the Plymouth around and driven it back in the direction from which it had come because Aunt Mary had been on her porch when she saw Gil's car approaching. At first, she thought he had forgotten something at home, but then the car passed by and at great speed. Gil didn't drive that way. She said the strangest feeling swept over her.

"Twenty-four hours later, the federal kidnapping statute was invoked and the FBI set to work. In the confusion, Aunt Mary neglected to check the mailbox, and when she finally did, she found a type-written ransom note. There was no postage, and it was assumed that the note had been placed there by the kidnapper just prior to the abduction. Under guidance of the FBI, the family tried to follow his instructions. Cash was brought to the designated location, but no one showed up. It quickly became clear that we were dealing with an incompetent criminal. He had no plan to get the money without getting arrested and we found out later that he lived in a rented room and had no place where he could have held my uncle without fear of being observed. In addition to the cruelty, stupidity was another dagger. The two make for a particularly dangerous cocktail.

"The kidnapper was already known to the police. He was a thirty-year old drifter from Wyoming with a record for petty crime. He had recently arrived and worked part-time work locally. I won't say his name." The Heiress paused.

"I like that part about not saying his name." said Lauren Campbell. "You know I saw a talk show, a forum on gun control. Someone called in from Sweden to say that over there, you cannot publicize the names of the accused, only the convicted. By then the interest has usually worn off, and killers don't get much publicity. I think that's a great idea. You can take away their guns, but when away their publicity, it might be even more effective."

"You make a good point." said the Physician. "However, I'm not so sure it applies to this case. The killer was known, but still at large. In a case like that, publicity can lead to a capture. Look at the success rates of some of these crime shows. Also, while publicity can be a motivator, it's not clear what was going on in this guy's mind. He made literally no effort either to get ransom money or to get away with the crime. All he did was run. He was probably antisocial. But he may, who knows, have felt so faceless, so doomed that he just wanted to get the suspense out of the way."

The Heiress went on. "The police found a typewriter in his room and it was determined to be the same one used to write the ransom note. So now all they had to do was find him. Pictures of the kidnapper were widely circulated by the police and the press. The family made pleas on local television. We had a candlelight vigil at Trinity Lutheran and it was moving to see that hundreds showed up. The kidnapping had shattered the community's image of itself, but the crowd was also due to the fact that Gil was also loved and admired. Later, there were searches with many with many volunteers. It was the biggest effort ever in Wisconsin; but they didn't find him.

"Then, almost a year later, hikers found Gil's skeletal remains in a wooded area about ten miles from the crime scene. He had been shot several times. The killer's trail remained cold for another six months until someone who had seen his picture in Reader's Digest alerted the Royal Canadian Mounted Police that someone who looked very much like him was staying at a Winnipeg rooming house. When the police came to his door he said 'I give up. I'm the man you want.' He died in prison a long time ago."

"Thank you for a very nice story." said the Physician. "It's not a nice story; it's a moving story. I apologize. That's just me; I still have some of the old Brooklyn habits in me. If these jokers are planning to make a gesture of so-called good will by releasing one of us, then it should be you. You've been through enough."

"Aren't you here without your medication? If so, you may be in danger. I think it should be you."

The Physician waved her off. "Nah, I'm an old guy. You're a young kid with your life in front of you. You should go first."

The Physiologist's Tale

At that point, the baton was passed to the Physiologist. "I have a story to tell. I'm afraid it's a return to the old theme of personal grievance, but I feel strongly about it and it's not directed toward anyone in this room. This is the story of an Internist, an academic physician. As a scientist working in a medical center, I was always acutely aware that these guys had all the power. This Internist was a guy who liked to… well, you'll see.

"At the front of the university hospital where I once worked, near the pick-up zone where patients are delivered in wheelchairs to waiting cars, there is a traffic island planted with palms and segos and just the suggestion of a path across the mulch made by the few people who cross it as a shortcut. It isn't much of a shortcut. It doesn't save much distance and that's probably why the path is only slightly worn.

"One who used that shortcut the Internist and he was very much a creature of habit. Every morning, he would step out of his sparkling clean BMW and on his way to the front door of the hospital, he would glance at the sign that read Doctor's Parking Only and he would smile because he knew he was one of the privileged. He would cross the pavement and then the traffic island in strides that seemed just a little too long. He was a man in a hurry; a man with purpose, always looking at his watch.

"His crossing of the traffic island is very important to our story at hand, but let me tell you a little bit about our hero, and he is a hero in the end, though he won't seem so at first. He was a man with a thoroughly forgettable face and he carried a host of insecurities. The Internist acted, *acted* I say, as if he truly believed that being an academic physician made him both a smart and important person. He was constantly finding verification of those beliefs in the way others treated him and he was never above pointing it out whenever he could. He was overheard telling a patient who had asked his first name, that his first name, the one on his birth certificate, was actually Doctor. He liked to describe himself and his fellow physicians as 'the best and the brightest'. In other words, he wanted to have those accolades by virtue of membership in a club, rather than by earning it as an individual. Suffice it to say, he was not actually among the best and brightest. When asked to help out with a clerical task, like putting together an address list or handing out brochures, he might respond. 'For this I went to medical school?' He once proposed at a staff meeting that tasks for an upcoming conference could be assigned according to a list of 'people whose time is very important, people whose time is important and people whose time is less important'. Of course, the people whose time was 'less important' were sitting right in front of him and he didn't hesitate to name them. That shocked everyone at the table. The door to his office was plastered with "my daddy the doctor" pictures that he had no doubt carefully instructed his children to draw. He was completely transparent and completely unaware of his transparency. The Internist had hard-shell finish, the one that made him impervious to the disrespect of others. All this made him an interesting figure to study and to trade stories about, and many did so.

"At the time our story begins, the Internist had a problem. He was not funded, meaning he did not have a research grant. He had been insulted by the Chair of Medicine, a red-faced, swarthy man with a black beard who, in Draconian fashion, had cut by ten percent, the salary of the Internist and other faculty members who had no research grant. The Chairman had a Napoleon complex, but a little bit of Googling reveals that he is actually a little shorter than Napoleon. Napoleon was five feet tall, that's five French feet, which by the way works out to five-six and a half English feet. In other words, he was of average height for his time. By contrast, the Chairman was an even five-four.

"The Internist felt the salary cut as a bigger blow to his ego than to his wallet. As a result, he didn't complain about what the Chairman had done, but rather he tried, unsuccessfully, to keep it quiet. Then he found a solution. There was a Pharmacist named Judy whose job was coming to an end. She was in her late fifties and the sole support for an alcoholic husband who also had medical problems and did not work. She had an idea to save her job. She had sketched out a plan for an innovative study and she hoped a drug company might fund it. If obtained, such a grant would provide several more years of salary support for her. She presented the idea first to the Internist for a couple of reasons. First, not having a Ph.D. or M.D. she could not be the Principal Investigator on any grant, but she knew that the Internist needed a grant and did not have one. Second, the Internist had an ongoing relationship with the drug company in question. And so, all told, she had good reason to think the grant might be funded. She wrote the grant entirely herself, but it was submitted solely in his name and to the pleasure of all, it was funded. After the money arrived, the Internist realized that he could get a graduate student to do the work for free. He had sole financial control and so he got rid of the Pharmacist. And here the story is vague because after she left, she lost touch with all of us at the med center. So, we don't know what happened to her, but it can't have been good. With this incident, the Internist's antics had turned from benign to malignant. The Internist got his full salary back but his reputation took a big hit. But in true fashion, the Internist seemed impervious to the gossip that swirled around him.

"On a fateful morning nearly a year later, the Internist had just left the doctor's parking lot and was crossing the little traffic island at the front of the hospital when his foot sunk to the knee in the soft sandy soil and became stuck. He brought his free foot up beside it and began to strain, but could not free his stuck foot, which was quickly saturated with ground water. Suddenly the ground gave way under both feet and he dropped straight down into a hole, briefcase and all. It was a big drop. He was shaken up, but not hurt. Now he found himself in the pitch dark and ankle-deep in water. Where he stood at the bottom, the chamber was much wider that he could have spanned with his hands. But the opening to the sunlight above him, the opening that was well out of reach, was just wide enough for him to have passed through. It was like he was standing at the bottom of a bottle that was almost empty. In fact, he was inside a typical Florida sinkhole. Once his eyes adjusted to the darkness, the circle of light above became blinding. He knew there were people passing close by, but he could see no sign of them. The Internist called out until his voice was hoarse; still no one heard him. His cell phone didn't work in there. As the morning passed, the sun rose higher and a little more light came down into the hole below where he waited. Exhausted, the Internist sat down in the shallow water. Slowly his attitude was changing from outrage over the indignity that had been served to him to the realization that his life might be in danger.

"By the time the light inside the hole had already reached its brightest and was beginning to decrease, that is the late afternoon, the hole on the surface had in fact attracted some attention. Someone shined a flashlight down inside. He did not see the Internist, who again could not make himself heard. Several more returned and blocked the area off. The Buildings and Grounds Director for the University decided to fill the sinkhole with concrete.

"As it was starting to get dark, a concrete truck arrived and its deep grunting and churning resonated within the sinkhole. In a growing state of panic, the Internist recognized the sounds. Now there was noise and it would be even harder to make his voice heard. Suddenly it became pitch black when the concrete chute was placed into the opening of the sinkhole. Concrete came down the center and there was splashing all around. The Internist pressed himself against the side of the chamber and used his briefcase to shield himself from the torrent of concrete and the spray of grey water issuing from its sides. As concrete filled the floor of the chamber he struggled to keep himself on top of it but also found himself sinking into it. Finally, the concrete and the noise stopped. A steel measuring tape was passed down into the hole and quickly removed before the Internist had a chance to grab hold of it. The concrete truck had stopped churning and in the eerie quiet he could faintly the voice above him 'Fourteen foot more, brother. Let's call it a day and do the rest in the morning.'

"That night, the sinkhole made that local news. There was footage of the concrete truck. A hospital official told the viewers at home that once filled, the sinkhole would not pose any kind of threat the hospital. No one had any idea that there was someone down inside.

"Needless to say, the Internist spent a cold and miserable night. He was afraid to sleep and he was covered in cold sweat imagining the possibility waking up embedded in hardened concrete. If that happened, the new concrete that would be poured in the morning would bury him alive. Then halfway through the night, two rainbows rose above him.

First, he realized that the concrete was beginning to set and that he could stay on top of it. He might even be able to lay down and sleep a little before sunrise. Second, he realized that he had an umbrella in his briefcase and that he could put it to good use. He took the spokes apart. He tore up the fabric of the umbrella and used the strips to bind the spokes into a long pole. He attached his favorite blue and white Johns Hopkins tie to one end and raised the pole through the opening to the outside above. It stuck out a good foot or two above the opening. Surely the workmen would see it in the morning.

"As the Internist sat with his back against the wall of the chamber and his legs stretched over the hardening concrete floor, a wave of exhaustion passed over him. Then did the dark night of his soul truly begin. He saw above him, a glowing mandala. Within each section of it, a sordid little scene played out. The bright wheel of his past deeds turned above him and at first, he did not recognize the man he saw. But the delay in recognition proved useful because the Internist was filled with pity and disgust for the small man who tried to cover his insecurity. That man was suffering! Could no one see? He was suffering because he had no one to share his thoughts with. But what was the man actually doing? He was trying his hardest to make *sure* that no one else could see. As he watched, he was overcome by the foolishness of it all. Then he began to see the parts of the story that he had never witnessed in the world above. It was so dark he could not see his own hand in front of his face. He heard the gossip that followed him. He saw the anger and disappointment in Judy, saw how she imitated and made fun of him behind his back. The realization that the man he was looking at was himself came over the Internist by degrees, and as a result was not so hard to accept. It was almost like getting into cold water gradually. Soon, he began to find it the feeling stimulating. Then something truly amazing began to happen. The Internist had true insight. He began to form a plan that he would put into action as soon as he was above ground. He was now sure he was going to be rescued.

"By the time the concrete truck arrived, the Internist was truly happy. One of the men had gotten out of the truck. He noticed the tie on the end of a pole. 'What is this?' He tugged at it and the Internist tugged back. 'Holy shit! Someone is down there.' Soon enough they had a ladder down the hole and the Internist came climbing out. He wore a gray suit of concrete water. The fine grit permeated his skin and hair. Otherwise he was alive and well. He was taken inside the hospital, where he was warmed and bathed and shaved and given IV fluids. That evening, from his bed, the Internist saw his case covered in the local news. He saw a file photo of himself and he was identified, not as a doctor, but simply as any employee of the hospital. His first and last name were given, no title. That hurt him, but just a bit. Immediately the Internist noticed that something was different. The failure to be recognized for his status created just a twinge, a momentary pain that passed quickly. It was not the searing and stinging wound that such slights had caused in the past. His plan was already working.

"Upon release, he did a little detective work and he found Judy's address. Next, he sold a good part of his stock and obtained a check for an amount equal to the of salary that Judy should have received from the grant. At first, she didn't want to see him, but quickly realized the seriousness of his purpose. The Internist handed her the check and said, 'This really should be our only interaction.' Judy quickly agreed. 'We won't be going out for coffee, but the score is settled now and I will always remember you for this.' And with that, the Internist walked outside into the mild November sun and he realized that he had never noticed before what a pure and valuable thing the sunshine was."

"Whoa, whoa, whoa" cried the Physician, who had been squirming and blanching throughout the entire story. He held up his characteristic stop sign. When he does that, the right palm opposes the flow of offending words while supported at the wrist by the left hand. This makes for a stop sign that is stronger and harder to run over.

"Hey, hey! Not fair." he continued. "What exactly do you have against physicians? Medicine is an essential part of life. Look at the group of us here in this room. We're not exactly spring chickens, and that is no doubt due to the fact that back at the disco, they intentionally chose, from among us, mostly those who they thought might have money. But on principal they will never get a penny from my family. Here's my point. How many of us in this room owe their lives to medicine? How many have had pneumonia or survived cancer or in some other way survived an illness that surely would have killed them had they been born just a hundred years earlier. Can we get a show of hands?"

"No show of hands needed." said the Physiologist. "I totally get your point. But here's my beef, not with physicians as a whole, just with a subset. There is a certain insecure type who craves external validation for his sense of intelligence and importance. There are some who grant that kind of respect automatically and naively to all physicians. Some of them get that free pass, while the rest of us have to earn it. That's what these types are looking for. It goes without saying that I don't include you in that group. But those others, like our Internist before his epiphany, they're impostors, four-flushers. Don't get me wrong; there are many PhDs who are just as bad or worse, the difference being that they don't have the same power. They don't get the same advantages or as much credit."

The Physician appeared somewhat mollified by this answer, but he was still visibly upset. Adrenaline, once released, cannot be called back so easily. He was silent for a moment. He looked distressed. Then he turned pale and slumped over, much to the concern of all. Within a minute, the episode had passed and he was beginning to feel better.

"That was a heart arrhythmia" he explained, still pale and wiping the sweat from his brow. "I get them from time to time, and here I am without medication. Without that medication, each episode is a role of the dice. Could be nothing, as it was this time. Could be fatal. You just never know."

With that, the Physiologist jumped up and confronted the Gentleman Terrorist. "This man needs medication. What are you going to do about it?"

"Does this look a pharmacy to you? He has already made his need clear. If I had the drug, I would certainly supply it, as he may yet prove to be a valuable asset. You, however, may be under the impression that you, meaning all of you, are here for your own good. Let me turn that question around. How much concern do you have for *our* welfare?"

"We don't even know who you are."

"Exactly my point. But soon enough, the world will know."

Where Did the Ski Bum Go?

The next morning, The Ski Bum was not present at breakfast, not in his sleeping bag, and not in the bathroom. Where had he gone? At one end of the hall were several doors that were locked and barred from the other side. That is where the terrorists spent a good part of their time. He had to be in there. But why?

There was talk among the other hostages. Were the terrorists giving him drugs? And why would they do that? The Gentleman Terrorist had been observed paying a lot of attention to The Ski Bum.

Elytra said "I knew him back at the Mount Lasser Resort, or I knew of him; that's more like it. He was a part-time ski instructor and part-time gigolo; mostly women, a few guys. I used to see him with them at The Tubes. They say he has quite a coke habit."

"He's definitely showing signs of withdrawal from drugs or alcohol." said The Physician. "I'd offer to help except that he's none too friendly and I don't have access to medications, so I really couldn't help him anyway. I tried to talk to him. He won't talk."

The Sergeant-at-Arms cut in "Somebody asked why these scumbags would give him drugs. I'll tell you why. Old Frenchie is obviously sweet on him. Puppy love; now isn't it just darling?"

He added "I call him Frenchie, but I think he's more like a generic foreigner. I think he doesn't actually come from anywhere in particular. Look at him. He looks just like the Sphinx."

The Physiologist thought for a while about the puzzle of The Ski Bum. He kept picturing the familiar look; the downcast gaze, the eyes like eggshells, dilated and empty, the blonde hair hanging in his face. The Physiologist was aware that he himself sometimes had a downward gaze and he quickly digressed by recalling two painful incidents in which he had been mocked for it.

In the first, he was about ten years old and lost in thought as he walked the mile or so to the library. He stopped beside a driveway to watch ants streaming out of an anthill. In a trance, he moved closer and used a stick to divert their stream. As he did so, a car full of teenagers pulled up slowly behind him and they blasted the horn. He had nearly jumped out of his skin. He had been a target for bullies. In most cases, they targeted kids who were small, funny looking or who act strange. None of these were the case with The Physiologist. They branded him as an outsider because he seemed detached from the group, because he seemed vulnerable that way, despite his having a strong social instinct. In contrast, he imagined The Ski Bum as having had early social success in the form of high school popularity. As the Physiologist remembered his childhood, he realized he was not simply lost in thought, but depressed as well, although he could never have put that thought into words. He was depressed over being falsely branded as an outsider. He was also powerless to do anything about it, as his inner world was overpoweringly attractive and he was not about to give it up. The Ski Bum was depressed too, but The Physiologist guessed it was for an entirely different reason. The Ski Bum didn't suffer from being branded by others. His failure was real.

The Physiologist remembered another incident, this one recent and with a happier outcome. As an adult, he had learned to handle himself better. He was walking down a sidewalk on the campus where he worked. He was in his private universe, so it was natural that his eyes were cast down as he walked. As one detaches from the real world, it is necessary to look down so as not to misstep. But looking down was still something that made him vulnerable to the prying eyes of those who do not understand or respect introspection, that is conformists. As The Physiologist walked by, a groundskeeper working in the bushes had called out in mockery. "I don't know what you're looking for, but you aint gonna find it down there on the sidewalk. Haw haw!" The Physiologist was, of course, angry at the insult, but he didn't know how to respond, so he just walked on. The next day, he was walking the same sidewalk with a co-worker when he was lucky enough to have a chance to even the score. He saw the same groundskeeper trimming hedges and he told his companion "Just play along with me and I'll explain later." So, his companion followed the Physiologist as he went up to the groundskeeper and pointed at him. "There he is! That's the guy I was telling you about. This guy thinks he can insult a complete stranger for no reason." The groundskeeper knew very well what he was talking about and he shot the pair a guilty look. He began slapping his own thigh saying "My bad. My bad." The Physiologist point a finger and told him "Don't let it happen again."

An hour or so later, The Ski Bum entered through one of those doors at the end of the hall. Someone could be heard bolting the door behind him. The Ski Bum was looking up and smiling. He looked refreshed.

The Sergeant-at-Arms sang out "Well, well, well. Where ye been Billy Boy, Billy Boy? Where have ye been, charmin' Billy? I believe you've been to see someone in the manner of a wife; a young thing who cannot leave her mother."

"We're not havin a conversation, Flattop."

"I always did wonder about old Frenchie. Seems a little light in the loafers, what do you think, Fulton?"

"I think you better shut the hell up, man."

"Don't be so hard on the Gentleman. He's only doing what all brave sailors do when they're far away at sea."

The Ski Bum looked different. He looked refreshed, confident. He looked straight ahead. His hair was out of his face. "They were interrogating me, OK."

"Why would they do that? You don't know shit."

"I know a washed-up asshole when I see one."

With that, The Sergeant-at-Arms lunged at The Si Bum and was quickly restrained by several others.

The Ski Bum added "Who are you kidding, old man? You may have been a tough guy at one time, but right now you've got some high mileage, a gut and too many flatterers licking your boots. Soft living has caught up with you for sure."

The Psychologist got between them "It doesn't help us to be at each other's throats."

The Ski Bum continued "The leader is an educated man. He wants us to know that he intends no harm. He is not an Islamic terrorist. He is a member of a separatist movement. His people want to govern themselves. They want to be free of Indonesia."

The Sergeant-at-Arms minced back at him "Is that so, pretty boy? They're not really our enemies? Then why are they locking us up? Why did they kill all those people back at Mount Lasser? I know! They must have different customs; different ways of expressing their friendship. I guess my *cultural sensitivity* could use a little work."

What The Ski Bum said didn't add up and, what's more, he didn't really seem to believe it himself. He had a little smirk on his face. Nothing was explained, nothing cleared up. There was tension in the air that was bound to flare up again.

Operation Haystack

Meanwhile on the other side of the world, a dossier had been assembled for each hostage. While the public knew only the number of hostages, but not their names, the FBI kept the families of the hostages well-informed about the investigation and also warned them not to negotiate with the terrorists if approached. By the President's orders they were to pay no ransom. Among the hostages, four came from wealthy families and would have made good targets for ransom. The Osterberg family was worth over a billion dollars. Members of the Neurologist's family had made a fortune on the stock market. The Sergeant-at-Arms truly was worth the fifty million that he claimed. The Executive was worth twice that.

By far the most important piece of information obtained by authorities was that the Navy Pilot had had an experimental tracking device implanted in his calf. At fifty, Lieutenant Captain Richard Neudeck had retired as a navy test pilot. He had flown virtually every type of plane the Navy had to offer except sea planes. During the last few years of his career, Neudeck had been granted extended leave to pursue his interest in mountain climbing. He had been a member of a team that had climbed several mountains in the Himalayas. Richard Neudeck had also volunteered to be part of a Navy program for testing advanced tracking devices. Having the device implanted would have had obvious appeal. Mountain climbers often carry tracking devices which serve both to aid rescue efforts and to verify that the team has reached the summit. The device in Neudeck's leg had a greater range than other devices and that was overkill, but it sure made Neudeck feel like a big shot. The device was classified, but its price tag alone would have made it unavailable to the public.

The device was developed for the military because of its potential in locating persons whose position is known with only a low degree of precision, for example a pilot forced to parachute behind enemy lines. The device contains a small chip about the size of a grain of rice and is programmed to emit a regular signal. It is powered by a battery that is recharged by physical activity, much in the manner of a self-winding watch. Of course, a pilot can simply carry a tracking device in his gear. However, the implanted device has the advantage that it is still operational after the soldier had been captured. The Navy Pilot had a faint, white hairline scar on the back of his calf, one he did not show to the other hostages when they were all comparing scars.

The distance at which the signal from the tracking device can be read depends on the method of detection. The maximum distance is fifty miles with an ultra-sensitive detection device mounted aboard reconnaissance aircraft. However, it was not possible to surveil the entire earth in a fifty-mile grid. What was also needed was a rough estimate of what part of the world the hostages were located. A break came with the arrest, in Houston, of two members of a sleeper cell for an Indonesian separatist movement. Captured computers revealed knowledge of the planning of the attack on The Tubes. A phrase in the Tetun Dili language indicated that they might be somewhere in the eastern part of Indonesia. But Indonesia is made up of seventeen thousand islands spread over three million square miles of ocean, so the task ahead was still daunting. This information was confirmed in an unusual way. The Chameleons were recorded that night back at The Tubes. During the band's break, which is when the raid took place, one of the mics was accidently left open. The recording captured a few phrases that were also identified as being in Tetun Dili.

President McKelly was determined to make the key decisions regarding the hostage situation himself. Within hours of learning about the tracking device, he called General Richard Mars at Robins Airforce Base outside of Macon, Georgia and assigned him the role of leading the effort to locate the hostages. General Mars was head of the 12th Airborne Command and Control Squadron operating the E-8 STARS Program of ground surveillance aircraft. The aircraft were capable of detecting the signal generated by the device in Captain Neudeck's leg as well as producing detailed ground imagery.

The next afternoon a meeting took place in the general's office. His office was austere with the only decorations being his West Point diploma and a picture of the President. The one extravagance was the table in the adjoining conference room which the general had had constructed from a large Southern cherry cut from his parent's property in North Florida after the death of his father. Five sat at the table: the general, the chief designer of the tracking device and three officers from the E-8 STARS program who would begin putting the plan they would form into action. A number of considerations came into play. It was important to locate the tracking device without the terrorists knowing that we had done so. Otherwise, they might have time to disarm the device and move the hostages. The tracking device did not produce a continuous signal; that would be wasteful of energy and would exceed the ability of physical activity on the part of Captain Neudeck to keep its battery charged. Instead, the device was designed to emit a signal every fifteen minutes. With that in mind, it was important to design the surveillance grid in such a way that the signal could not be missed. The E-8C aircraft would provide ground imagery as well, but that might not prove productive because the terrorists were likely to keep a low profile. However, they might have had trouble hiding the jet that they had used to cross the Pacific. There was also some concern that the E-8C aircraft is large and fairly easy to locate from the ground. However, it flies as 38,000 feet and this dramatically reduces its visibility.

A decision was reached to deploy a team of E-8C aircraft from Anderson Air Force Base on Guam. And so, Operation Haystack was born and a team of reconnaissance planes began the arduous task of surveying from all of Indonesia, from Sumatra in the East to the Solomon Islands in the west; from and from Malaysia in the north to the Islands of the Timor Sea in the South.

Old Fitzgerald

On the seventh morning, the group sat down for their morning meal as usual. The Heiress was not among them. She was not in her bed and there was no one in the bathroom. Of course, there was wild speculation about where she might be. Released? Killed? The Gentleman was not present and the two young soldiers, no more than boys really, who served their meal did not speak English. So, no information was available.

After breakfast, the Psychologist spoke over the din of conversation "Good morning. Today, I'm going to tell the story of Old Fitzgerald, a remarkable man in many ways. It's also a story that I saw, in good part, with my own eyes, starting at the age of six, growing up in Eastern North Carolina. Of course, Mr. Fitzgerald had a first name, but I never knew it at the time. We kids were raised so polite back then that we rarely knew the first names of adults. It was Mr. and Mrs., ma'am and sir. And if we did know their first names, we passed them around among us and dared to imagine that we might greet adults with phrases like 'Hi, Bob' or 'Nice to see you, Joan'. It was a time and place where the differences between adults and children were exaggerated.

"The year was 1964. We had just moved into our neighborhood, one that was developed by the Fitzgeralds. Our house at 30 Mary Lane was a split-level with cocoa brown asbestos shingles above and white clapboards below. It was a thing of joy for our young family. Mary, I later learned, was Mrs. Fitzgerald's first name. It was an exciting time and I was just old enough to remember exactly how my parents felt. Daddy had come from poverty. He had a master's degree and had risen to a good job with the State. We were on the upward arc. We had a gang of kids to play with, more or less the same age and we were constantly in and out of adventures together. It was a happy time. Our subdivision was just outside of Coinjock, a town of no more than half a dozen stoplights."

"Coinjock, are you serious?" the Musician cut in.

"Yes, Coinjock is real. It's my home town. Look it up when we get back home."

"Coinjock! I love it. Now let me ask you this. Does the name refer to an athletic supporter made from coins welded together? Or was the jock only meant for *holding* coins? I like the first explanation better, but inquiring minds want to know."

"I have no idea where the name came from." The Psychologist was smiling. "The early sixties were a time of low curiosity. I don't remember anyone ever mentioning the subject."

"So, it stays a mystery, just like Pigeon Forge."

"Pigeon Forge?"

"Tennessee. Pigeon Forge is that county-western destination. They advertise it as a resort, but the most I can honestly call it is a destination."

"Hey, I resent that." said the Sergeant-at-Arms. "I been to Pigeon Forge and it's a nice place."

"Nice and corny. My point is that some say there was a forge where they made iron pigeons and others say the blacksmiths were actually pigeons. Once again, I don't think we'll never know."

The Sergeant-at-Arms glared at the Musician.

The Psychologist smiled again. "When our neighborhood was subdivided, the unpaved road that had once ended at the Fitzgerald house was made into a loop, leaving them on a big island that was shaped like a teardrop or perhaps in hindsight you might say a hangman's noose. The road could have been paved, but the Fitzgeralds liked it the way it was. They were old-fashioned like that.

"Mr. Fitzgerald was an electrical engineer and long before he became Old Fitzgerald, he founded an electrical contracting company that eventually became the biggest in that part of the state. Around the Fitzgerald house were a total of twelve homes, built over the course of just a few years. Mr. Fitzgerald built some of them with his own hands and the help of a crew. Other lots were sold off to developers. The back of our yard bordered on Hatchet Creek and on a summer day, we often walked it all the way down to Fishs Eddy and swam there.

"In the summers, we used to drive out to the Outer Banks. Back then it wasn't packed with McMansions on stilts like it is today. There just a few small towns and miles of empty beach. Jim and I ran down the dunes at Kitty Hawk holding out our wings and pretending we were the Wright brothers. I liked to collect that yellow-green sea weed, the kind with air pockets. I would walk along the beach popping it. When I popped one right behind Daddy's ear, it caused him to swerve. He pulled right over to the side of the highway and threw my sea weed out into the brush.

"I want to say the Fitzgeralds were about ten years older than my parents. They were the natural leaders of the neighborhood and they had a reputation for generosity. They had an enormous garden and they gave away most of the vegetables it produced. All of us kids help a little with the weeding and a lot when it was time to pick. There was bursting white corn, tomatoes bigger than a softball, okra, eggplant, watermelons, pumpkins, lettuce.

"Mr. Fitzgerald was sometimes home during the day and we kids would flock to his garage to see what he was up to. On Saturdays, especially, we would watch him in the woodshop. With great patience, he would show us each tool and how to hold it. He had a sawmill rig and he made furniture from Southern Cherry, cut and aged right on the property. He showed us how the wood was sawn and how the trunk was fit into the carriage. Then he would have us stand back while he sawed a plank or two. The blade was as wide as a truck tire and after it stopped whirring he let me touch it and feel its warmth. I remember watching him make a beautiful china cabinet with beveled glass. As each step was successfully completed, he was increasingly all smiles and muttering "yep, yep, yep" to himself as he worked. Watching Mr. Fitzgerald was an inspiration. Most of us dream of doing all kinds of things. But procrastination is such a part of most of us, even when we are in the dreaming stage, we imagine doing things at some day, maybe far in the future. Not Mr. Fitzgerald. He would set to work right away. He worked so fast that you could almost see his project, often a piece of furniture, come to life right before your eyes. Mr. Fitzgerald was also the kindest man I knew.

"We did have one small disaster. Mr. Fitzgerald was burning some brush and he had cut up some poison ivy vines, as thick as my wrist, that had growing up the side of an oak tree. He wore gloves as he worked. He showed us how to identify poison ivy and warned us of its dangers. What he didn't know is that the poison ivy oil is volatile and is released into the smoke when it burns. All of us got terrible cases and spent the rest of the summer covered in calamine lotion.

"The thing I remember best of all about the Fitzgeralds was their Christmas displays. It started with a sleigh full of presents on the roof, complete with Santa and the reindeer. Lights were stung around Santa and the reindeer and along the sled runners. And of course, there weren't the flashing lights that we have today. I remember a couple of things that confused me as a child. First, the display on the roof was actually put up by Mary Fitzgerald's father, whom we knew as Mr. Roth. My older brother Jim said it was exceptionally kind of a Jewish man to put up a Christmas display. Later I learned that he was a Christian and that his name was spelled R-A-U-T-H, not R-O-T-H. The other misconception I had stemmed from the Christmas carol with the words 'up on the rooftop, reindeer pause'. I kept looking up at the reindeer on the Fitzgeralds' roof and thinking that can't be right. Bears have paws; reindeer have hooves.

"Those displays got bigger and better every year and soon they were drawing families with small children from far and wide. The paper would tell you where all the big displays were and the Fitzgeralds always headed the list. People joked it's a good thing he's in the electric business. With all the kids assembled and just as it was turning dark, Fitzgerald would light up the display, one element at a time, just to amaze their eyes. There was a Santa and reindeer on the roof and four or five more in the yard. Then, out in the woods, there would appear various reindeer on the loose or a giant snowflake. Over the years that I watched those displays grow and grow to the point where it was almost like daylight in the Fitzgerald yard.

"Then one day everything changed, and here I'm getting to the crux of the story; there was a terrible accident on the highway. Mel Lazenby, one of Fitzgerald's foremen, was at the wheel of the pickup.

Mr. Fitzgerald was in the passenger seat and Mrs. Fitzgerald was in the seat behind him, in the extra-cab, as they called it. They were on state road 431, rounding a long curve, when a car came straight across the center line and struck them head on. Each vehicle was estimated to be going around sixty, so that's quite an impact. Mary Fitzgerald died at the scene. Mel Lazenby was driven beneath the steering wheel and into the space below the dashboard. As his thigh struck the brake pedal, the pedal snapped off and the J-shaped pedal arm was driven deep into his leg, an atrocious wound that is so much worse even than being stabbed to the hilt with a Bowie knife. Mr. Fitzgerald was not wearing a seatbelt and he was thrown through the windshield, his body striking a telephone pole. The telephone pole had, for some strange reason, a spike driven into it that stuck out several inches. Fitzgerald's forehead was driven onto that spike. The head of the spike penetrated his skull and also prevented him from falling. In a most horrible way, he was left hanging from the spike, with his toes barely touching the ground. The girl who was driving the compact that hit them, Saskia Williams her name was; she was also killed. The truck ran right over and flattened her little compact, leaving her trapped inside like a sardine in a tin can.

"The ambulance attendants went first to Mrs. Fitzgerald and quickly determined that she was dead. Mel Lazenby was responsive and did not begin losing a lot of blood until they took him off that brake pedal arm that was driven into his thigh. Once they got him into the ambulance, they went to take Fitzgerald down from where he was hanging and they were amazed to discover a pulse. I think the Grim Reaper must have been on coffee break when it came time to dealing with Mr. Fitzgerald that day. It took several hours for a special crew to arrive and cut Saskia Williams out of her car. She was dead by the time they got her out, but she may have survived a good part of that time. That possibility, that likelihood, has significance, as I'll get to a little later.

"Mel Lazenby appeared at first to make a good recovery, but then blood clots began to catch up with him. Eventually, they would kill him. The large veins of his right leg were entirely clotted and the surgeon removed the massive clots, which they say came out in a shape that was branched like a tree. In the process, the valves in those veins were lost. They were stripped out. As a result of losing those valves, the return of blood to the heart was poor and Mr. Lazenby's right leg blew up to nearly twice its normal size. Nevertheless, he soldiered on bravely for a while and ran Fitzgerald Electric while Mr. Fitzgerald himself recovered.

"Then the parents of Saskia Williams made things infinitely worse by suing Mel Lazenby for wrongful death. Saskia Williams was a junkie. Her two children had been taken from her a long time before and placed in foster care. Know why? Because her parents were unfit, too. Saskia Williams had nodded off at the wheel that fateful day. However, her blood tested negative for narcotics and that finding complicated things. Fact of the matter is that something unusual can happen when a person dies slowly with heroin in their system. As I said, she may have lived for hours while they were cutting her out of that wreck. Daddy worked for the State Toxicology Lab and he explained this to me; much later, not at the time. If the person dies slowly, narcotics may be transported out of the blood and into the acidic contents of the stomach. The coroner tested her blood for narcotics, but not her stomach contents. If he had done so, he almost certainly would have found heroin there. Unfortunately, this was a local investigation and State experts were not consulted.

"In order to support their lawsuit, the Williams presented their daughter as a responsible young mother and the victim of an alcoholic. Mr. Lazenby was known to drink some, but had not been drinking at the time of the accident. The Williams' alleged that the pickup crossed the center line and killed their daughter. They harassed that poor man as he lay dying in his hospital bed, wheezing away his last breath with his lungs full of blood clots. That's unforgivable. Luckily, the day was saved by an alert motorist who had stopped to help and finally came forward with pictures of the accident scene. Shockingly, the police never photographed the scene. I guess that goes with the half dozen traffic lights I mentioned before. Those photos clearly showed the position of both vehicles and the all the skid marks. And they proved beyond question that the pickup had never crossed the center line. It was in fact the compact that had done so. The case was dismissed.

"During the next months, Mr. Fitzgerald began to make a remarkable physical recovery and that is also when he first became Old Fitzgerald in my mind, as you will soon appreciate. It was a while before we were allowed to see him and in turn, we all went to pay our respects. Fitzgerald had been a strong and vigorous man. Old Fitzgerald was gaunt and pale. He had aged so much. They say he had hallucinations of smell. His face would twist and contort with shocking suddenness when the hallucinations would come over him. People would ask him what it smelled like and he would say like nothing you've ever smelled. It could not be described. That first morning he spoke to me so nicely. I remember his exact words. He put his hand on my hand and said 'Thank you for coming to see me, little Claudia. I have all of your get-well cards on my dresser. You know it's those cards that helped me get better.' When I repeat it, it sounds like something nice that the familiar Mr. Fitzgerald would have said, but coming from Old Fitzgerald now, well he sounded like a robot. I was scared, but I wasn't scared off right away. His eyes had always been such a mild green. But now, at certain angles, they would show a glimpse of the intense green you see at the edge of a sheet of plate glass, and at those times, he looked a million miles away.

"Pretty soon, we kids established our old habit of coming to observe what him at work around the yard and garage. He could walk and use his hands perfectly. His stamina was slowly returning. But sometimes he would snap at us for no reason and send us all home. Our parents said we should try to be understanding. My parents also said that at Dave's Dairy Freeze, Old Fitzgerald pinned a man against the wall because he thought he had cut in line. Toward summer's end we noticed that the garage lights were often on late at night and sometimes we could hear him in there yelling and throwing things. The neighbors were talking.

"By Christmas, we found out what he had been working on. Old Fitzgerald announced that there would be a Christmas display that year, just like any other. But it would be a smaller display, one he could set up by himself. We were all assembled on the Fitzgerald driveway that first night. As it grew dark, he flipped a switch to illuminate a hanged Santa. A sign pinned to his chest read 'Santa was depressed this year'. He flipped another switch and we saw another Santa standing on his sled, and peeing on the reindeer, as represented by a string of pulsing yellow lights. Next, we saw Santa cut off the head of a reindeer with an electric chainsaw. Fake blood was spurting everywhere. Finally, we saw Santa inject himself with drugs and slowly turn blue. Then Old Fitzgerald barked at us "Show's over. Go home." After that, and needless to say, I was not allowed to go to the Fitzgerald house and the same was true for the others. But Old Fitzgerald still had an audience for his sick little show for another couple of nights because there still people who came in from the outside and didn't yet know what had happened.

"That cruel Christmas farce was Old Fitzgerald's declaration of war against the neighborhood. A crew came and installed a steel fence around the perimeter of the teardrop island. As soon as it was finished, Old Fitzgerald could be seen posting no-trespassing signs along the fence. The McKisson's beagle got onto Old Fitzgerald's property and was killed in a bear trap. Fitzgerald returned the dog's body and admonished them to respect his posted signs. Mr. McKisson exploded 'What are you doing setting traps in a residential neighborhood? And what's this about signs? Don't you know that dogs and little children don't read?' Fitzgerald was silent and smug. Mr. McKisson threatened legal action, but that didn't work. Fitzgerald had retained the biggest lawyer in the area and all his moves were planned with legal advice. One of Old Fitzgerald's own miniature pigs got out and into a neighbor's yard. He apologized to the neighborhood by crucifying the pig on a small cross at the edge of his property. Of course, by now all kids in the neighborhood were strictly forbidden to go near the Fitzgerald property. And of course, we spent a lot of time looking through that fence. We might have created a whole mythology about Old Fitzgerald except we didn't have to. The reality itself was so strange that it didn't need embellishment. One night, Mother said at dinner 'We have to get Jim and Claudia out of this neighborhood.' And so, we did move, and not too much later. We moved to Raleigh, where Jim and I finished high school. I hate to drop the ball here, but after we moved we didn't learn a whole lot more about what happened to poor Mr. Fitzgerald.

"The story of Old Fitzgerald has always haunted me. It marked the beginning of my interest in psychology. To me, the story represents a fundamental challenge to the way we see ourselves. Instinct tells us that we essentially create ourselves, that we mold our own character, taking freely and voluntarily the advice and example of those around us. But this story argues that at least to some degree, we are the product of outside forces. It argues that we are not acting, but acted upon. The story evokes this fear in me and that is why I think it has had a lasting impact on me.

The Neurologist spoke up "I have a brief thought on that if you have the time for the ramblings of an old man."

"Please go ahead." Said the Psychologist.

"If the spike entered Fitzgerald's forehead, it probably damaged a good part of his frontal cortex. As a result, he would lose the ability to inhibit his impulses."

Lauren Campbell objected "Yes, but those impulses were so hostile. Where would they come from in a man who had always been so exceptionally kind?"

"Ah. The hostile impulses are actually a part of normal psychology. What is abnormal is only the inability to suppress them."

"I'm afraid that's right." added the Psychologist. "When we meet someone for the first time, we may notice that they are fat or ugly or seem stupid, but if we're normal we certainly don't say any such thing. We need the vigilance of our frontal cortex to suppress such urges. Look what happened to poor Mr. Fitzgerald when that wasn't working."

The Physiologist added "That's the physical argument, and it's pretty clear-cut. We all like to think we are the captains of our own fate, we have a natural instinct to believe that, but we also know sometimes our will is overruled by external forces. Your story about Old Fitzgerald is an example of that and it's pretty convincing. That's the physical question; but here's the metaphysical question and it's one that I think is more interesting, interesting in a way. I'm not really so sure there is an answer to it or even that the question makes sense. Yes, we are sometimes the product of external forces, that is for sure. But are we *ever* anything more than the product of external forces? Are we ever the product of our own free will? If the answer no; if the answer is that we are just a piece of flotsam on a raging river beyond our control, most of us would find that answer pretty disturbing. Most of us are glad to be normal and not, say, a serial killer or something terrible, but is that any of that our own doing or are we just lucky? The idea that it might be luck is disturbing."

The Neurologist "OK, what is your metaphysical question?"

"The question is this: is our cherished concept of free will real or is it an illusion? If all that exists in the universe is governed by the laws of physics as we know them, or even roughly as we know them, then the short answer is that free will is an illusion. But now take a closer look at the question. If the events of our lives are preordained, then so is everything. Everything, including the instinctual belief that everyone has in their own free will, is preordained. That is a circular argument, a reductive argument, an 'is what it is' argument. In other words, the question doesn't really mean anything. But there is still a nagging question: where does free will come from?"

"Now you're getting into deep water." Said the Physician.

"Don't worry I'm not going to drown. I'm just going to have a nice little swim."

"I think I'll stay on shore." the Neurologist laughed.

"Do as you please, but you might want to jump in at some point because some of this might piss you off."

"Do you enjoy pissing people off?"

"No, but I'm not afraid of it either."

"OK, OK. Whatever." The Physician waved him off.

"OK, here's my point. Where does free will come from? The laws of physics describe a chain of cause and effect. But the concept of free will requires breaking that chain. It requires changing the path from what might have been to something else, specifically something that we hope is better. But what force is there outside the laws of physics? None that we know of. But just because we don't know of something, does that mean it doesn't exist?"

"There's the deep water I was talking about. What you seem to be talking about is an article of faith."

"Just the opposite. Thinking that all you see is all there is; now *that* is an article of faith. Respect for the unknowable aspects of life is enlightened. By the way, there are two kinds of things we don't know. There are the things we know we don't know. They don't present a serious problem. But what gets us in trouble are the things we don't know we don't know."

"OK, smart guy. First, I'm not in trouble and second, what exactly is it that we don't understand?"

"In a word: consciousness. Consciousness cannot be explained by science."

"That's where you're wrong. Consciousness results from electrical currents generated by firing neurons. There is a lot of work being done by neuroscientists in this area."

"Here's the part that I thought might piss you off. When of chain of firing neurons produces a measurable effect, it can be explained without any need for a concept of consciousness. Neuroscientists cannot explain consciousness because they cannot observe it. The only consciousness any of us can observe is our own. But this observation of our own conscious creates the possibility of a force acting outside of what we normally call the laws of physics. It's only a possibility. We don't know and we never will know."

Things were getting a little heated at this point, causing The Psychologist to intercede. "Now boys, I'm not going to take sides, but I will say this. I think the story and the ensuing discussion has taken us far away from matters at hand. And that has to be a good thing."

Clay and Sandy

That same morning, the Gentleman came in and sked how they enjoyed their meal, while radiating a most insincere smile. He enjoyed anticipating their questions.

"Yes. You are most observant. You have no doubt noticed that we have released one of your number as a gesture of good will."

"Good will and a dune buggy full of cash, or whatever it is you all drive." charged the Sergeant-at-Arms.

"If you think you are in the middle of the desert, perhaps you are not so observant after all." And with that, he bowed ceremoniously before departing.

After the Gentleman was gone, Lauren Campbell spoke up "I'm going to tell a different kind of story today, one that I think is uplifting. We all could use that; I know I could. This is the story of Clay and Sandy, how they fell in love, how they were forced apart and how they came back together.

"For many years, Sandy lived next door to me in Florida. She was and still is my best friend. Her story is one restores my faith in human nature. I hope it will do the same for you. At the time that we moved into the neighborhood, Sandy had been married to Tom for about ten years. Sandy was not particularly happy in her marriage. There was nothing specifically wrong. There was no fighting but there wasn't any real communication either. Over the years they had drifted apart. They couldn't have children and it was probably just as well.

"Tom was cold and a little superior. I didn't really like him. And I really never got to know him, although we spent a lot of time together as couples. He was always checking his watch or his cell phone. He gave the impression that he would rather be somewhere else. I found it unsettling. Sandy would often confide in me. She'd say, 'He's not interested in companionship, he's barely interested in sex, he has no hobbies. He is being swallowed up by his job.' Eventually, Tom and Sandy divorced.

"One morning, when I was over for coffee, Sandy brought out a box of high school memorabilia. Most of the items in it had to do with her high school romance with Clay. Sandy's parents had both been teachers and they ran a waterskiing camp during the summer. The camp was very successful and always drew a handful of rich kids from as far away as Europe. Clay was a star skier and held a state high school record for jumping. They put on several shows every season for the parents and for local charities. Clay and Sandy had been in these shows together. She showed me the flyer from a Wild West waterski show that listed both their names; Clay as a jumper, Sandy as a driver.

"Also inside the box were two tri-fold posters on Florida geology that she and Clay had made for Earth Science class. Clay's poster was on the Hawthorne Formation, a geological area of North Florida made up of sand, red to orange clay and phosphate rock that can be mined as fertilizer. Clay had gone with a geologist to visit an abandoned phosphate mine and he had attached to the poster samples of rock and clay plus several small fossils; shark's teeth and what looked like part of a turtle shell. There was a map of Florida, showing the Hawthorn Formation in red. There was also a diagram showing how a typical creek bed cut through the formation, revealing fossil shark's teeth as old as ten million years. Below the diagram were pinned several fossil shark's teeth that Clay had found in creeks near his neighborhood. They were combinations of grey, black and tan. Some were smooth, some serrated.

"Sandy's poster was about beach erosion. One panel showed photos of the beach and route A1A at Flagler before and after a hurricane. Another showed an aerial view of a rock jetty with sand accumulating on one side. There were pictures of Miami Beach 1930s vs. present-day, showing how much smaller the beach had become. There was a sandwich bag filled with fine white sand from the Gulf and one with coarser yellow sand from the Atlantic.

"There was also a little poem the Clay had written for her in seventh grade. I still remember it.

THE SUN

> I like the sun; it gives me light
> Do you?
> I see you as the morning bright with dew
> And now we have the day before us
> We have our song, both verse and chorus
> And every note of it rings right and true
> I like the sun; it gives me light
> Do you?

"A green velvet box held the ring he had given her. 'Where is Clay now?' I asked. Sandy had no idea.

"By sophomore year, Clay and Sandy were dating and by junior year, they were deeply in love. Both sets of parents were opposed to the relationship; both thought Clay and Sandy were too young. When they announced their intention to marry after high school, both sets of parents were alarmed. Sandy's parents, particularly her mother, were adamant that they not see each other. The parents were successful in breaking up the couple only because Clay and Sandy were so obedient and because neither had the use of a car.

"Sandy's mother was he ringleader, calling Clay irresponsible and not headed for a good career. Sandy calls those misgivings manufactured. She said that her mother's own parents had married too young themselves and were not well-suited. They were projecting their own problems on their daughter and trying to cover up chaos in their own lives. Despite a calm façade, secretly, her parents were not getting along and their opposition to Clay and Sandy gave them a united front. Sandy's mother, who today in her late eighties is not totally clear, denies having forcibly broken them up and insists that all she did was advise against their wedding plans."

The Physiologist broke in. "I have a mother like that. In junior high, I was being picked on mercilessly, especially by one kid. I begged my parents repeatedly to go talk to the principal, but they wouldn't do it. One day as an adult, I mentioned to her that I had been picked on as a kid. She acted shocked and outraged and said to me in a very blameful way 'Why didn't you tell me? I would have done something about it.'"

Lauren continued. "Well, Clay and Sandy were effectively split apart and they lost touch with each other when Sandy went away to college and Clay went into the army. As I mentioned before, by the time I came on to the scene, Sandy's marriage to Tom was wearing thin. After ten or twelve years together, they had an amicable and uncomplicated divorce and each went their separate ways.

Then, a couple of years later, something amazing happened - and here I'm getting to the point of the story. Sandy was on a trip to of all places, Seattle, Washington. Far away, is what I mean. She turned a corner and there was Clay! They both stood frozen for a while because that was how long it took each of them, first to recognize and then to believe. They sat down for coffee and here is what they discovered. Both were recently divorced with no children.

"Sandy also learned that after he got out of the Army, Clay went back to school and became a nurse practitioner. He now worked for a company that supplied emergency medical helicopters. When a hospital bought one on these helicopters, Clay would travel to that city and spend as much as a month there, teaching the staff how to perform emergency medicine on a helicopter. Sandy's parents had been wrong about Clay. He had a better job than her father ever did.

"One thing led to another and now they are back together. Sandy moved in with Clay and they married. They have a beautiful house. It's a modern cracker style, kind of on the small side with heart pine floors. The front yard is taken up almost entirely by a giant live oak that could be, who knows, five hundred years old or more. The limbs are horizontal and covered in thick resurrection fern which turns brown in dry weather and springs back to life after it rains. However, the lower limbs are so shady and the bark is so thick and holds so much water, that the ferns stay green most of the year. The north side of the trunk is covered with the most beautiful pink and white lichen. Around the tree, at the perimeter of the yard is a ring of dichondra ground cover."

"And then what?" demanded the Lawyer.

"That's it. Maybe you expect something terrible to happen. Well, that's just not the case. This is a true story with a happy ending."

The Event Planner's Tale

"After, hearing Lauren's story, I've got to tell you mine. You know I'm an event planner and I planned a wedding that took place last summer at Mount Lasser. It's a very popular spot. I made a point of coming back to ski with my husband Jeff, who is back there now. I'm afraid he must be more worried about me than I am about myself. I like to think of myself as an optimistic person, but back there in California, back in the US, what do they really know of our situation?

"The wedding was an open-air ceremony for about two hundred, followed by a reception in The Tubes. It was a beautiful wedding. It should have been; the parents of the bride certainly paid a small fortune for it. Judging only from the way things turned out so well that day [there was a lot of good will] no one could have guessed that the wedding of Sanjay and Jenna almost didn't take place at all. I got the scoop from Jenna's friend Alyssa over a few glasses of red wine.

"As the reception was winding down, my job was mostly done. She was sitting next to me at the bar. The bartender asked her, 'Another Malbec?' and she nodded.

'I'm Alyssa' she said. 'I'm Jenna's bride's maid.'

'Petra, the wedding planner.'

Alyssa whispered. 'Have you noticed something about Jenna and Sanjay, something about their physical appearance?'

'Not especially.' I said. 'I mean they are a nice-looking couple.'

'Go take another look. She's supposed to be Anglo and he's supposed to be Indian and yet they look like they could be brother and sister. Don't you find that surprising?'

'She's blonde…'

'Bleached.'

'OK.' I told her. 'Listen, don't go anywhere; I'll be right back.' Anyone who knows me knows I love gossip. I was excited.

"When I got back, I told her. 'Honey, what you're saying makes sense. Tell me more.' I noticed her half-glass of wine was now full again.

"She was all lit up. 'Now that I have your attention, I'm going to tell you the whole story from the beginning. The two families, the Dykehouses and the Muraladhars were neighbors going way back to before any of the children were born. Sanjay's parents are Sunita and Samir Muraladhar. The Dad goes by Sam. Sanjay's little sister Vena gave that stand-up comedy slash Broadway musical routine that she did for the couple. That's, I understand, is a very Indian thing to do. Ben and Barbara Dykehouse are Jenna's parents. Anyway, you know these people.'

'Yes, of course. I made all the arrangements and the Dykehouses paid for it.'

'OK, now to set the table…Jenna and Sanjay were playmates in the neighborhood from the time they were very small up until I think it was maybe the seventh grade. That's when then Dykehouses moved to another part of Stockton. After that, Jenna and Sanjay were in different neighborhoods, different schools. They didn't see each other. Cut to junior year when they're re-introduced at a party. They spent the entire evening in a corner talking about old times and soon began dating. Jenna tells me that right from the beginning, her mother tried, gently at first, to talk her out of the relationship. She would say 'He isn't right for you. Nip this right in the bud before it gets serious.' Things like that. And since it happened more than once, Jenna would protest 'Why don't you like him?' The answer was 'Oh, it's not that I don't like him. I do like him; he's a very nice boy. I just don't think he's right for you.' Barbara, the mom, denied that there was any ethnic basis for her feelings, but the remained vague about the actual basis for her objections. Vague, but persistent. Sanjay was getting the same kind of pushback from his father, Sam. Jenna and Sanjay were very perplexed by all this. Neither parent could cite any good reason all for their disapproval. This seemed to leave ethnic prejudice as the only possible explanation. But Sam Muraladhar is very Americanized. He will argue pro football with you all day and night. Likewise, Jenna said she did not think her mother could be prejudiced. The odd thing was that her Dad, Ben, and his Mom, Sunita or Sunny as she was sometimes called, seemed perfectly OK with the relationship.

'Throughout their junior year, Jenna and Sanjay's relationship was progressing rapidly and they were seeing each other a lot more than their parents knew. They were falling in love. Love conquers all; that's what they say. But *their* love had to climb a mountain higher than Mount Lasser. You'll see.' Here, she started to tear up a little.

I put my hand on her shoulder. 'Don't be upset. They reached the top and so will you. Your day is next.' I knew without having to be told that she was a little wanting in that department. I could tell that most of her friends were now married except for her.

Alyssa went on. 'Toward the end of that junior year, Jenna and Sanjay called a family meeting at which they announced their intention to marry after the completion of high school. The meeting did not go well. The upshot of the whole thing was that Jenna was sent out of state to private school for her senior year. In the meantime, all four parents took harsh measures to keep them apart. They were only partly successful.'

I said 'What is this all about? I'm dying to know.'

'Well there was another meeting, a meeting of just the parents this time. Sam and Barbara revealed something they could not say in front of their children. The two had had an affair many years ago and Jenna was their daughter. The argument that followed, and you can imagine it was quite an argument, was at first all about the betrayal. But then an even larger issue emerged. I got all this from Vena, who was supposed to be in her room with the door shut. Sam Muraladhar was pacing the room. 'He kept saying, shouting really, 'You don't get it. You just don't get it. The affair is over; long over. We both regret it. What's done is done. This is not about betrayal; this is about the law. Sanjay and Jenna are half- brother and sister. I am the father of both. It is against the law for them to be married. We have to forget our differences and do the right thing here. This wedding can't go forward.'

'Oh, my goodness.'

'But it's still not what you think; that's the crazy part. You'll see. Jenna and Sanjay endured the end of the school year and the beginning of the summer, restricted by curfews and seeing very little of each other. Finally, their parents told them the truth and of course Jenna and Sanjay were devastated. Jena started her senior year a Calistoga Academy, a boarding school two hours away. But by this time, there was no need for a forced separation. They were half-brother and sister. The relationship was over.

During this time, a great deal of tension building up within Sunny Muraladhar. She called another meeting of the four parents where she made a startling announcement. 'Sam, there is something I've been holding back. I'm sorry to tell you that you may not be the father of Sanjay.' Sam was again, pacing the floor pounding his fist into his hand. She said, 'You are a fine one to talk about betrayal.' He softened a bit and said, 'What do you mean, you are not sure?' 'I mean I cannot be sure, but by appearance, he is not yours.' And so, a DNA test was performed and it showed clearly that Sam is not Sanjay's father. Jenna and Sanjay are unrelated after all and so the wedding could go forward. Now you're asking, 'Who *is* Sanjay's father?'

'Yes.'

'Sunny will not tell. She insists that is only Sanjay's province to know, and so far, he doesn't want to know. Now, in the space of just a few short months, something remarkable happened. The parents set their differences aside. Jenna and Sanjay rekindled their relationship. A stigma like thinking you are half-brother and sister is not easy to shake off, but they did it. And so here we are today with a happy ending. Here's to Jenna and Sanjay.'

And with that we clinked glasses and drank up."

The Release of the Heiress

At 6:41AM on the following morning Egyptair flight KE237 from Nairobi touched down at Athens International Airport. The captain made an announcement first in Arabic, then in English. "Attention, please. Due to a special security situation, when the aircraft has come to a stop, all passengers must remain in their seats. I will notify you when you may get up, retrieve your overhead luggage and deplane. We do not anticipate any extended delay and we sincerely apologize for any inconvenience."

While the announcement was being made, the Air Marshall escorted a bedraggled passenger off the plane. He held up his badge, took the passenger by the arm and brought her directly to the customs desk, where he demanded to speak to the chief customs officer. They were taken to a private office. "The passenger with me claims she is an American hostage taken prisoner in the terrorist raid that occurred just over a weeks ago in California. She has no passport and no identification of any kind."

"Who are you and how did you get on the aircraft without a ticket or identification?"

"My name is Carol Osterberg. I am an American citizen. I have no identification because it was taken from when I was abducted as you have just heard. I think I was brought onto the flight by one of the terrorists. He must have had some paperwork. This is not the first plane I've been on in the last twenty-four hours. They took me from my bed in the middle of the night. It must have been last night."

"You *think* he brought you onto the plane?"

"Yes, I woke up part way through this last flight. I must have been drugged."

To the Air Marshall "Who is this man who may have brought her onto the plane? Did you encounter him?"

"Yes. He brought the passenger onto the plane in a wheelchair. He wore a Kenyan Police Service uniform and showed me extensive paperwork indicating that he was transporting her as a prisoner who was being extradited to Greece. Here's the part that is slightly embarrassing. I let him slip off the plane before we left Nairobi."

"A slight embarrassment that will no doubt cost you your job."

At this point Carol Osterberg spoke up. "There is a simple was to prove that I am telling the truth. Take a picture of me and send it to the American Ambassador. He may not know who I am, but he can verify it through Washington in a matter of minutes."

"You are smart. You are smart. Yes, that is exactly what I will do."

Within a couple of hours Ambassador Roger Czenski arrived at the customs office, accompanied by two armed guards. On the ride to the American Embassy, the Ambassador did his best to assure Carol that her ordeal was over and that she was now back in the American sphere of influence. As they stepped out of the black limousine, the very appearance of the Embassy building seemed to provide reassurance. The building was a landmark, designed by famed Bauhaus architect Walter Gropius, a symbol of power and prestige.

Carol handed a sealed envelope to the Ambassador. "This is a message from the terrorists."

"I see that you did not open it."

"I touched it as little as possible, knowing it may contain forensic evidence."

"Good. I'm glad you managed to conceal this from the Greek authorities. That's actually pretty lax on their part. I'm not going to open either. I'm going to let the FBI do that."

Soon Carol was receiving medical attention within the Embassy. After two days of observation, she was cleared for transport back to the US.

The message in the envelope stated that Carol's release was gesture of good will and not the result of a ransom payment. There was a demand that, for the release of the remaining hostages, ten billion dollars be paid into a bank account for which the number was supplied. The note also demanded the release of four individuals currently being held in American prisons. The President slammed his fist on his desk. "First, they've killed how many Americans, Jim?"

"One hundred and eighty is the current count, Mr. President."

"Thank you. Now they want more money to finance killing more Americans. Let's see if that bank account number is real. I wouldn't be surprised at all if it wasn't. That's how much chance they must know they have of getting even a nickel out of us. Here's the part that gets me. How was the family that Osterberg woman able to pay ransom money right under our noses? I want to know how that happened."

Carol went on the Today Show to tell her story and to deny the allegations that were swarming. She appeared with her parents and their long-time family lawyer. It would appear that the choice of the Today Show was based on a guarantee of soft-ball questions. That is certainly what they got. Carol told the audience she did not know the identity of her captors and did not even know where she had been other than somewhere in the tropics. She reported that she and the others had been treated well and she told the story of her release and arrival in Athens. The lawyer said that the family had had no contact with Carol's captors and that her release may have been a gesture of good will toward future negotiations and to a family that had already been touched by tragedy. The parents told the story of her uncle's kidnapping and murder and photos from that incident were shown onscreen.

As a result of this broadcast and various news reports plus all the endless panel discussions of twenty-four-hour news television, public opinion was split. Some thought the Osterbergs had endangered American security, others understood why they had done what they did. In the end, the government decided not to pursue a case against the family.

The Musician's Tale

It stormed through the night and into the next morning. All night, rain lashed against the high windows and drummed against the corrugated roof. Gusts lifted a part of the roof that had detached and when they subsided, the roof slammed back down onto the concrete block. There was water on the floor. Hardly anyone had slept a wink. At breakfast, it was still dark. Occasional flashes of lightning illuminated the sleepy faces.

Altogether, rain and thunder made a great din and the Musician struggled to be heard above it as he addressed the group. "Today, I'm going to tell yawl a right salty tale. Salty in two ways: one because it is indeed a sea-faring tale and two because of the salt of tears, as ye soon shall see. A tale full of storms it is, such as ye see about. This tale is made all the sadder by the fact that every word of it is true. But before I begin my tale, I must make use of the best advice my Pappy ever gave me. He said son, it's always good to keep your audience waiting. That's a little bit like saying that it helps if the food critic is hungry when he visits your restaurant. Put it another way..."

"Quit farting around and tell your story." said the Physician.

"Now hold on just a second, there, young fella. I haven't even started my delay tactic yet. So here it is. I would like to keep you waiting for the story by first making a pitch for the power of rock and roll lyrics and hitting you with a little quiz on the subject. This winner gets this". [the dried, baseball-sized husk of a tarantula that he found in the building]. The Musician throws it into the middle of the group.

"Oh my god, are those things here?" said the Psychologist.

"I think they're cute. Now in my view, a good rock lyricist can reveal the essence of who he is in just a line or two. Here a few of my favorites. If you don't flat-out know who said it, I'll bet you can figure it out.

First quote 'Please don't spoil my day; I'm miles away and after all, I'm only sleeping.'"

"Easy. Beatles."

"OK, but *which* Beatle?

"John, of course."

"Quote number two 'I guess I'm just like a turtle, hiding underneath this horny shell.'"

"That's my girl Janis" the Sergeant-at-Arms bellowed.

"Number three 'In searching for a meaningful embrace, sometimes my self-respect took second place.'"

"David Bowie."

"No. Anyone? Actually, it's Iggy Pop."

"Four and five come from the same group. Four: 'In living, I've been tossed about by every she-rat in this county' and five: 'My name is gorgeous purple and I'll shake my mane and rail against the Queen and all her servants.'

"Stones."

"Numero sies: 'Sugar plum fairy came and hid the streets, looking for soul food and a place to sleep.'"

"Walk on the Wild Side."

"Lucky seven. 'My thoughts are scattered and they're cloudy. They have no borders, no boundaries. They echo and they swell, from Tolstoy to Tinker Bell, down from Berkeley to Carmel. Got some pictures in my pocket and a lot of time to kill.'"

"Mr. Paul Simon. I saw him in 2018 on his last tour."

"How do you say eight in Canadian? 'I wish I had a river that I could skate away on. I wish I had a river so wide that I could never reach the other side. Oh, I wish I had a river I could skate away on.'"

"Joni Mitchell."

"Number nine? 'Find my nest of salt. Everything's my fault.'"

"Curtis Interruptus. Curt Cobain; gone too soon."

"Realms of bliss, realms of light; some are born to sheer delight. Some of us will share the light. Some are born to the endless night.'

"Doors – Morrison."

"Eleven and twelve are from the same source. 'Once in a while you get shown the light in the strangest of places if you look at it right. And another: 'If you get confused, just listen to the music play'

Silence. "Anyone? Anyone? [The Musician imitates the sound of a buzzer]. OK, that that's Grateful Dead lyricist Robert Hunter. Now tell them what they would have won, Don Pardo."

Two more. Let's try to get these. 'Everyone was against him cause the cat might be a little bit different.'"

 "Hendrix"

"Here's the last one. I could go on; there are so many. 'Last night I saw a cowgirl come floatin' past me 'cross the ceiling. Last night as I closed my eyes, I saw a *naked* cowgirl on the ceiling. But when I went to follow her, I could not move; my legs they had no feeling."

"Anyone?" Silence. "That last one was a toughie – ZZ Top. And by the way, I might have embroidered a few of those along the way.

Anyway, nice job, class! You people are heavy [flashes the peace sign]. You answered correctly for ten out of the fourteen. But guess what? You're still in detention! Hah hah! Just ask that guy over there" [pointing to the Gentleman Terrorist]. The Musician looked pleased with himself. It may have occurred to the Gentleman Terrorist that he didn't seem to be reaching this the Musician.

The Musician controlled his giggling and continued. "And now, after hopefully exhausting the patience of everyone in this room, it's time for me to take up the story at hand, one I call 'The Voyage of Captain Cookies.'

"We open on a crispy October evening in old Liverpool, back in the sailing days. Under a full-masted moon, the camera zooms in on our hero, a funny little fellow named Hootily Tootily Pollutily, who incidentally, looks a lot like Stimpy. Action. We observe Hootily as he comes spilling down the back steps of a bordello. At his side, he has his equally-intoxicated and faithful companion, Senor Bacon Bits. Illuminated by a street lamp, down on the shiny cobblestones of Paradise Lane, Senor Bacon Bits helps his friend to his feet and also helps him dust off his slightly dented sense of dignity. Hootily curtseys coyly in appreciation.

"Our two boys have been given the boot for insufficient funds. And they never did obtain any favors from the fine ladies inside, although they did gorge on free snacks in the parlor, so the evening was perhaps not a total loss. That parlor, and I can picture it now, presents the viewer with a bit of a puzzle. With its player piano and its Wild West décor, it seems to have come straight out of nineteenth century America and yet our two heroes are from eighteenth century England. A mystery, to be sure. Many stories commit anachronism, but very few accurately predict the future!" The Musician doubles over with laughter, before regaining control of himself.

"On with our story. 'Does ye think I still look cutily?' asks Hootily Tootily Pollutily, furiously batting his false eyelashes.

'Absolutily.' his good friend responds in full support. And together, arm in arm, they stroll aimlessly down the darkened path of Paradise Lane. Then, without warning, invisible blackjacks strike each on the back of the head at the exact same instant, and soon there is a field of brightly twinkling stars around the head of each. Our friends are lifted by rough and unseen hands, placed into wheelbarrows and carted away.

"Your character Hootily —what is it?" said the Physiologist.

"Hootily Tootily Polutily to be exact."

"Thankyou. He reminds me of Stimpy. Which brings me to the question of what Stimpy is; human or dog. Ren is a dog, a Chihuahua. But what is Stimpy and what is Hootily, human or dog?"

"The answer to your question is yes. Now, where were we before I was so beautifully interrupted? In the foggy morning, first light finds the two asleep on the deck of the HMS Sea Hag. Under a thick blanket of sea smoke, they lay snoring. Now the Sea Hag, I will remind ye, she is a right unusual ship, as much so as any ye may ever see. She has two strong masts, fore and aft. But instead of being rigged with canvas sails, an enormous windmill cookie is attached to each mast. The gingerbread paddles, four to a mast, are edged and crisscrossed with lines of white icing and when the wind is a-roaring, why them paddles will spin so fast that a man had better watch his step, or else find himself knocked into the briny drink.

"Now beside a little shack on the forecastle, Captain Cookies is standing on a perch and pining for his faraway love, the beautiful Repulsinea. He has his trusty sidekick the Clown Loach swimming in the air beside him. At last, he breaks from his reverie and steps down to address his crew.

'Wuh? huh? Ahoy!' he says 'A fascinatin' dream indeed it was that I was havin'. Our ship a mighty vessel as she lay at port. Aye, many a chest overflowing with gold and jewels was displayed upon her deck by you, her sturdy crew. Her mighty wind panels stood tall, offering their ginger fragrance to all, their icing gleaming in the sun. Not a mark upon her steadfast hull. I saw everything I ever wanted and ain't no stinkin', grimy sea dog gonna stop me from getting it. Arrgh, I say.'

'Arrgh.' answer all the crew in unison.

'But first' says the Captain, 'I must seek the advice of me good friend Mario; make that Super Mario if ye please. Blazin' blue barnacles! What have ye there, Mario?'

'Mm-nhm-gmd-nm' he answered through a mouthful of meatballs.

'Mario it's good to see ye. I say it's good of ye to come aboard. Ye have the finest Italian restaurant in Liverpool. Tis a pity we cannot go there. I've come to learn that the whole town is covered in spots and so we must remain aboard the Sea Hag, in quarantine if you will. Now Mario, come to think of it, I could use your help. I had a dream, as I just told ye, where I was captain of a glorious returnin' ship. Well, I've decided to go after me dream. I got me a ship and a crew. I have a map and a route planned out. I have all that already, but I have no mission yet. Yet I do know it will become a most notorious voyage, whattaya say?'

'Mmmm, these meatballs are good, but they need a little more spice."

'If you like-a the spicy meat ball, then you like-a the spicy meatball. What can I say? So, it's off to the Spice Islands we go. Are you with me, crew?'

'Aye' all present answer in unison."

"Question, Ian". Said Elytra. "What are all these Italians doing in an English sailing story?"

"I have an answer for you, but you might not like it. Let's take an example. Suppose I'm putting together a recipe for spaghetti sauce to post on the internet. I might include an extra ingredient like horseradish on the theory that anyone who would put horseradish in spaghetti sauce gets what they deserve. But do you see how that leaves something important out of the equation? What if there are people who would actually like horseradish in spaghetti sauce? What if I happen to be one of those people? Do you see what I mean?

A crew member asks, "They got some spaghetti over there, eh?"

Captain Cookies explodes. "Have you been listening at all, ya bloody timber worm!? Be serious, man."

Mario cuts in "Hey, of course we all listen to you. You got the, uhh, special of the day or whatever. I gotta tell you, I don't like a' the fettuccini, but ahh... I think I come with you on the voyage."

And so, Captain Cookies is satisfied. "So, you'll be goin' with us then, Mario. Good. Let us be gatherin' the crew, then."

Captain Cookies then tells Mario, sternly "I need the best crew ya got here, one that will last through a rigorous journey."

With that, Mario heads back to his restaurant. He takes a look inside his Crew and Accessories Closest and returns with five able-bodied seamen, all named Mario.

Ever helpful, Mario replies "Well, your basic crew, she starts at about $300. From there, we go way up the elevator. My best crew is around $4,000. By the way, where's your bathroom?"

"Third door on the left."

So, the Captain, with his steady first mate Bag-O-Tea beside him, sets about examining his crew. The two soon discover that Mario has brought only one crew member. The crew of five are in fact, Mario in a variety of disguises, trying to get quintuple seaman's pay. Just then, their attention turns to the quarter deck and they look down upon our two forlorn heroes, Senior Bacon Bits and Hootily Tootily Pollutily.

"Why, what have we here?" asks the Captain.

"I say, look at what the tide brought in. These two appear good for exactly nothing, except ballast, perhaps." says Bag-O-Tea.

The Captain adds "I'm afraid you may be right, Bag-O-Tea." And now our two friends are really much dismayed.

Then Bag-O-Tea is struck with inspiration, as suddenly as if it were a bolt of lightning. "There's a mental institution nearby and I think we could find there at least 300 willing crew members."

And so, they set that plan in motion. But sadly, and due to a serious scissors accident, more than half are lost before even reaching the Sea Hag. The next step is to load her with provisions. That would be twelve thousand gallons of a mixture of honey, cottage cheese and African vodka. They arrange to meet back at the ship in two days to start the voyage. They christen the ship El Petredor [Spanish for The Loser] and set sail for Tahiti. But quickly, they remember that their ship already has a name – so scratch that.

The Captain beamed at his proud crew and asked, "Are we ready to draw anchor and set sail?"

Bag-O-Tea informs him, "Captain, we've already left."

The Captain replies, "Good work, Bag-O-Tea. I'm going into me cabin for the rest of the voyage."

After a few hours pass, Captain Cookies mumbles to himself, while looking at a map, "Hmm... sixty-two degrees west, put the right sail in- (Boom – he hears a canon firing) and shake it all about. Carry the decimal." (He hears a splash to starboard) "What the! Oh well. Turn north, and that's what it's all about." (Boom – more canon fire). "Mario! What's going on up there?"

"Is a launching contest, my Captain. "You oughta come up; its-a-pretty good."

Captain Cookies is now running across the deck. "What! In the name of all that is holy, stop this ridiculousness or I'll keel haul every last one of ye. We'll be reachin' land soon and we need to be ready. Bag-O-Tea! Yer the new lookout."

Bag-O-Tea replies, "Righto... Aye, Aye... Yes sir... Okie-Dokie, Smoky... At your service."

The Captain thunders "Get in the crow's nest ya worthless little."

Bag-O-Tea replied "Roger... Ten-Four... Will do."

Captain Cookies roars "Shut up and do it!"

Bag-O-Tea cautions him "Wait, captain. I think I see a storm abrewin'."

And indeed, there is a mighty storm acomin'. The sky turns dark and the wind kicks up and the windmills begin to turn. For six days, the storm rages. The rains are followed by hail. The sea turns a bright turquoise as if they are in the Caribbean, but instead, it's freezing cold. Ice floes come gliding past them. And standing on those floes are ghosts and beggars, dressed in bloody rags, laughing and mocking the crew of the Sea Hag in their misery. Every man aboard the Sea Hag is starving and at last they eat the gingerbread of their own wind paddles. Mountainous waves rock the Sea Hag. Her hawsers are tied to the dock, bow and stern, and the old dock, all grey with weather, groans as they pulled at her. Oh, wait, what am I saying? They're far away at sea. Never mind.

And when at last the storm has passed, the Captain bravely asks, "Mario, did we lose anyone?"

And Mario replies "Ahh, no, we no lose nobody. That storm, she was only 'bout a minute and a half."

Just then, Bag-O-Tea calls down from the crow's nest "Land ho!"

Captain Cookies valiantly addresses the crew. "Set the anchor, boys. Jacobs, Abraham and myself will take a lifeboat ashore. Bag-O-Tea, you go with Eliza and Kowalski. Repunzel, you stay here and keep the ship nice." Soon, they're in the life boat we hear their paddles hittin' the water.

Jacobs has to ask. "Doesn't this look a just little bit like home?"

Captain Cookies bellows with a confidence that reassures his men "Don't be fooled, lad. It's only a native trick. They set everything up to look like your home. That way they can keep us here and hunt us down later. It's just like insurance, see what I mean?"

Abraham is puzzled "But captain, there's Mario's Restaurant right over there."

Captain Cookies: "I already told ya. They know everything about us; they know just what will keep us here. But we're not staying. Just gettin' any treasure that may be here, then we're leaving, understand?"

Jacobs and Abraham answer together. "Yes, my Captain."

But the landing was a failure. They found no treasure, and they lost Kowalski to boot, or at least one boot."

Captain Cookies announced "Bad news everyone. There is nothing useful on the island. Let's move on toward Tahiti."

Repunzel responds "Captain, I think I got-a-more bad news. I'm afraid we've lost our provisions."

Captain Cookies demands to know "What!? How much?"

Repunzel clues him in. "We lost all of it... in a chugging contest."

Captain Cookies is furious. "Repunzel, I told you to keep the ship nice. That means no chugging contests. And also, don't let your hair down."

Repunzel shrugs "Hey is not so bad. I won the contest."

Captain Cookies is shocked. "Not so bad, is it? You idiot, now we'll have to return to England with nothing! Full about, navigator. Let's get this pathetic excuse for a crew back to their miserable home." And with that, the music of defeat begins to play.

And they sail and sail until Bag-O-Tea once again calls out "Land Ho."

The Captain is not happy. "Alright, we're back in England, now everyone get off my ship. You too, Repunzel, get off my ship." We hear the sound of their footsteps as they scamper like rats over the deck.

Then Repunzel cuts in "Ahh, hey captain. I noticed the ship, she's a-still tied to the dock."

Captain Cookies is piqued. "And why should I care about that?"

Repunzel has to explain it to him "Duh! Stupid! It means we never left."

"Stop" shouts the Captain. "You lie! This can't happen. We left here. I know it."

Mario tries to help. "Excuse, me. Captain Cookies?"

Captain Cookies replied "Yes, that's me, that's my name, but it doesn't matter anymore. We never even left port. (*laughing*) Doncha get it?"

On the dock stands an attendant from the Mental Institution. "Captain, they've been complaints. I'm gonna have to take you in with me."

In the final scene, our brave Captain replies. "Don't you see? I can't go with you; I haven't even left. Hah hah! You can't very well go if you haven't left, can you? (struggling) Hey! Get off me and get off my ship." His voice is fading as the captain is strapped into a straight-jacket carried away. "You can't fool me. I know your native tricks. Let go of me at once."

The attendant replied, "Man, it's a good thing there are guys like me. Otherwise people like Captain Cookies would be making voyages all the time-a. Well, I guess it's all in a day's work, eh? And so ends the story of the Voyage of captain Cookies."

Mrs. White interrupts "Young man, I find your story and as well as your music to be entirely frivolous. To think that I paid one hundred dollars back at the nightclub to hear what you call music. Ridiculous."

"I made two and a half million dollars last year."

"I can't imagine what for."

"That's right, you can't imagine. You have no imagination. You were born with it, but you've abandoned it."

"At least I don't go around presenting silliness as if it were music. I have that much dignity."

"Hey everyone, I'm ready to make an accusation. It was Mrs. White, in the bunker with the sharpened tongue."

The Physician's Tale

The Musician was followed by the Physician. "Hey, hi, good morning. How are you? Listen, I'm Ken. We've heard a good number of stories, OK? And it seems to me that their main intent has been to amuse, to enlighten, to titillate and, in one case, to uplift. Thank you, Laura for your lovely story about that young couple Clay and Sandy. Now, a good recipe should have a variety of seasonings. And in the same way, a good story should, I think, have a variety of angles, a variety of intents. I hope you will find in my story a little taste of each of the above, although I'm not so sure about the uplifting part, as you will see.

"The story I'm going to tell you is true. Not like the last one, this story really is true. It is drawn from my experience as an expert witness in the courtroom. I'm an academic neurologist, OK? That means I work for a University where I teach, where I do research and where I see patients. Over the years, I've trained a lot of people who have gone forward to make important contributions to what we know about the way the brain works. I was at Mount Lasser on a ski trip, although I do not ski. Why not? Because at seventy-six, I'm no spring chicken. Alright, so why was I there? As much as I can, I like to keep contact with my colleagues from the past, mostly young people who trained with me. Most of them are also doing research. This business networking thing that young people are so hot about, it's really important in science too, you know. Yes, I am getting to the point. It will just take a second more." He held up his hand to make a stop sign. No protests, please.

"Every few years or so, I like to foster this networking by arranging a ski trip. Each of us does a scientific presentation that lasts about an hour in which we talk about whatever it is that we are researching right now. The rest of the time is for skiing. There were eight of us plus four spouses on the trip. Four were in that crazy disco.

"My story involves an in-some-ways very talented low-life individual named Felix Catlanato who operated out of southeastern Massachusetts and who now resides in Framingham Correction Institution, also in Massachusetts. Catlanato was a local; he grew up in the area. In high school, he had been both a star shortstop and a minor juvenile delinquent, although it is possible he committed more serious crimes and just didn't get caught. He was well-built and had regular features. Now, most people would stop short of calling a man handsome when he dresses shabbily and frankly smells bad. Nevertheless, I would wager that, cleaned up, Felix Catlanato might look as good as a lot of movie stars. Catlanato owned a rambling business just out of town. It started as salvage yard, but soon expanded when he added a vegetable farm that he maintained on a couple of acres of imported topsoil. Next, he added a large greenhouse for growing roses and finally a store where he sold fruits and vegetables, roses and other flowers, local apple cider, prepared foods and various knick-knacks. With all of that plus the personality of a salesman, he turned Catlanato Salvage into a popular roadside stop.

"So, here's the story. I was an expert witness in a case against Catlanato. What that involved, we'll get into in just a minute. So, I'm up there in Massachusetts and I go out to his place of business, Catlanato Salvage just to nose around, not that I was paid to do that. The place is closed and all boarded up, of course. So, I'm driving out there to check it out, along Sheep Hill Road, I think it was, and I encounter something that really had me scratching my head. On a long, straight stretch of road with houses only on one side and marsh on the other, there is a stop sign at a place where there is no intersection. I just had to stop and knock on a door. I said, 'Hey, I'm not from around here. Do you know what this stop sign is all about?' Then I'm told that this is where a kid had been killed after running out from behind a parked car. Now, I'm thinking holy cow! I mean, don't they know that the next bad thing will be something entirely different? This closing the barn door after the cow is gone; it seems to be a universal human attribute.

"Anyway, I'm getting a little off the track here. I found out that many stories have been circulating about this Felix Catlanato and together they created for him the desired reputation, which was that of a man who was unpredictable, a man to be feared. One typical piece of folklore about Catlanato was related to me by a young man who was nineteen at the time. Over the summer he's doing yardwork for the for the Catlanatos at their house. One morning, while Felix is out in the garage, the young man has not started work yet and he's sharing a cup of coffee with Catlanatos wife Sherry, who was quite a piece of work in her own right and I'll get to her later if I get a chance. She's a stunning blonde, well-tanned, in her thirties, curvaceous and very flirtatious, smart, too. She's telling this young fellow all about her days as a crew member onboard a yacht that took high-end clients on sailing trips through the Caribbean. The kid can easily take various dates that she mentions and with a little arithmetic, figure out that she was doing this while married to Catlanato. He said that spooked him right off the bat.

"While Sherry Catlanato is speaking, she brings her face too close to his and she occasionally touches his shoulders. Later, when he's at work in the yard, she comes around to tease him again. She's wrapped in only a towel and she says, 'I'm going to be sunbathing on the other side of the house. I like to get a complete tan, so I don't wear a suit. Don't you *dare* come over there.' Wink, wink. Towards dusk, the kid has finished his yard work and goes inside the house, where he finds the couple arguing. He has arrived just in time to hear Felix Catlanato shout at her 'Fuck you, I'm going out.' Pardon me, but that's part of the story. 'Where do you think you're going?' Sherry asks. Catlanato has already passed through the front door when he turns around to tell her 'I'm going out to find some pussy.' Pardon, again. After Catalnato is gone, she says to the young man in a manner that shows a disturbing lack of concern, 'I hate it when he does things like that. I'd like to get back at him. Can you help me find a way?' And by then she has her arms around him. At that point, the young man freezes. Due to his age, he is of course full of hormones. By his word, he is not a virgin at the time, but he is not very experienced either. In contrast, she is, also in his words, hot as a pistol. At the same time, and speaking of pistols, he also knows that this was exactly how people get shot. Catlanato is unstable and has plenty of guns around. So, the kid does the smart thing. He just walks out the front door without saying a word and he never comes back.

"It turns out that Catlanato does not go out looking for women that night. First, he has a couple of quick belts at a place called The Lafayette and then he drives around for a while. He ends up near the shore, in the parking lot of Griffith's Seafood around 8:30, well after they are closed. He breaks in. He takes all the lobsters out of the tank and puts them in the back of his truck. Then he drives to his own place of business. Can you picture dozens of lobsters crawling and scratching around the bed of that pickup? The salvage place has a kitchen and he spends the entire night cooking those lobsters and picking out the meat. The following Saturday, there is a Fall festival at Catlanato Salvage and Felix is there selling lobster rolls. When Bobby Griffith catches wind of this, he rushes over and confronts Catlanato, who he finds wearing an apron and glad-handing a crowd as he sells the lobster rolls. Bobby Griffith challenges him. 'Where did you get all this lobster, Felix?' The answer comes back 'Seafood store, guy.' '*Which* seafood store, Felix?' 'What's it to you, guy? Can't you see I'm busy here, serving the people?' Felix Catlanato is grinning from ear to ear. Bobby Griffith doesn't go any further at that moment because Catlanato is a dangerous guy. But later he goes to the police and soon finds out they will not lift a finger.

"Now to the real heart of the story. One day, a cop is making a routine traffic stop along a lonely stretch of road down by the marsh. It's not late, it's around twilight, but there is no other traffic at all. So, what does this guy do when the cop comes up to his window? He shots the cop right between the eyes. Dead, instantly. There was probably a big argument first, but we don't know.

"The cop who was killed was young, he's twenty-five years old, well-liked, known to be a straight-shooter. He left behind a wife and two small kids. It's a big story, of course, and everyone is talking about it. Soon, it appears that the police are not making any progress in solving the case. The family grows frustrated, but they are told that there are simply no leads. The cop who was killed comes from a police family. In fact, his own father is also a member of the same local force. So, the father felt he was in a position to demand some answers, but he doesn't get any. Instead, he finds himself increasingly marginalized. At first, he thinks he might be imagining it, but then he was sure. All doubt is removed when he gets transferred. So, the family hires a lawyer and the lawyer could not get anywhere either. But this family does not give up; they are very tough. They waged a public opinion campaign with vigils, posters, appearances on local TV. After two long years, their diligence pays off. Seems the story has been gathering steam. As it should. The story of the murder of a policeman going unpunished because the police would not investigate is shocking. This of course, indicates some kind of corruption, but it's anyone's guess as to what the exact nature of that corruption might be. Finally, in response to public outrage, the governor appoints a special commission, the Kessler Commission, to investigate. They come in, they seize the evidence and take over the entire investigation and after that, the case is solved with incredible ease. The cop who made the traffic stop had written down the license plate number. The car belonged to Catlanato. Evidence as to his whereabouts at the time of the shooting checks out. Forensics shows the bullet came from Catlanato's gun. And there is other evidence too. Catlanato was arrested quickly. Open and shut case.

"Now to the most interesting part. The question has not yet been answered as to how Catlanato was able to suppress the investigation for so long. The answer surprises everyone. Turns out, Catlanato and his wife Sherry had been running a scam for years. She had slept with virtually every important politician in the area and he was two steps behind with a camera. There had always been gossip around town that she was a former high-end prostitute, whispered behind Catlanato's back as if he didn't know it. Boy, did he know it. The two of them had pictures and they had recorded phone conversations. They had made a lot of money blackmailing those politicians. Catlanato was very credible threat. They had used that money to expand the business, to buy a house in an upscale neighborhood and they took a lot of trips to Europe. When all this comes out, a number of prominent state politicians go down. Catlanato is charged with murder and blackmail and Sherry is charged with blackmail.

"Now, to back up just a little, I come into this at Catlanato's murder trial as a witness for the prosecution. That's where I usually end up because I've got this terrible habit, I have to tell the truth, and, as you probably know, the overwhelming majority of defendants are guilty. The defense claims that Felix Catlanato was not responsible for his actions, or has diminished responsibility, because he had a genetic defect known as Brunner syndrome. The claim is totally phony and it's my job to expose that. Without getting too terribly technical, Brunner syndrome was discovered about twenty years ago and there are only a few documented cases in the world. Men with this syndrome, and only men are affected, have a defective gene for making an enzyme called monoamine oxidase, or MAO. Without this enzyme, without MAO, they cannot break down certain neurotransmitters in the central nervous system. There has been a lot of publicity about this because people with true Brunner syndrome are very prone to violence.

"So, the defense presents the results of independent laboratory testing done with blood platelets obtained from the accused. They claim that these results show a very low level of MAO. There are so many things wrong with their claim. First there are two subtypes of the MAO enzyme. Subtype A is expressed in the nervous system, but it is MAO type B that is expressed in the platelets. Men with Brunner syndrome have a deficiency in MAO-type A only. Their MAO type B is normal, so the test is not valid. Second, the test that was done with Catlanato's platelets shows low MAO activity, but there is no positive control. In other words, it's not enough simply to show that his activity was low; you also need to test the platelets from one or more normal men, and demonstrate that they have a much higher activity. That wasn't done either. The results probably merely show that the assay was no good, conveniently and suspiciously no good. Most importantly, Catlanato's psychological profile does not match that of a male suffering from Brunner syndrome. Those with the syndrome display marginal intelligence, they are passive, they have few if any friends and their violent behavior is reactive in nature, meaning that their actions are not cold-blooded and premeditated, instead, they are reacting to a perceived transgression.

"Now let me contrast that picture with the perfect storm that made Catlanato what he is, and in turn, I'd like to compare both of them to Richard Kuklinski, The Iceman. You've heard of him? He's the most prolific mafia hitman of all time. I think the comparison is interesting.

"First, Catlanato. He is not of marginal intelligence; he is smart. He is not passive, he is aggressive and he displays considerable social skill. He is socially well-connected, although his associates cannot be called friends. They are simply people whom he uses. Catlanato has a love-hate relationship with his wife's promiscuity and ultimately with her. He is a latent homosexual. He seems to revel in her unfaithfulness, but only when he can justify it as serving his own ends. A complicated dance of denial. Catlanato comes from an abnormal background. His father was a thieving plumber who taught the boy a whole bag of deceitful tricks. The father also conducted cruel exercises to toughen the boy. When Felix started playing little league ball, the Dad said, 'I'm going to make a fielder out of you.' He bought Felix a new glove and then he would set the boy up in the garage for infield practice. The father had a box full of baseballs and he would throw them as hard as he could right at the boy's head and in rapid succession. The idea was 'You'll learn to catch if you don't want to get hit.' During that period, Felix would show up at school with bruising on his face, arms and chest. He would always claim it came from a fight.

"An important step in the development of a criminal is success, at a young age, in his experiments with violence. The principle has been well-described by Lonnie Athens. The average abuser starts out *being* abused, either in the home or by his peers. He is full of resentment and the desire for revenge. At some point, he strikes back at someone in a violent way and he is successful in doing so. Success is the key point. In the coming days, he may get a surprise. He is developing a reputation and is now treated with new respect. This can be an ominous change. Catlanato is rumored to have committed such attacks in high school. They went beyond winning fist fights. He is said to have broken a guy's arm with a two-by-four and to have set another kid's car on fire. Add to this that Catlanato is paranoid and that he needs to defend himself against not only real threats, but imagined threats as well. I'm sure he had some kind of manufactured, or half-manufactured beef against Bobby Griffith, although Griffith may not have known about it. None of that came out in the investigation. Also, Catlanato is somewhat deficient in another way. About one percent of the population is born with antisocial personality disorder. That means they lack empathy for others, that they are focused entirely on their own needs and cannot understand the needs of others. After learning as much as I could about Felix Catlanato, I do not feel that he has outright antisocial personality disorder, but instead, I think his empathy for others is a good deal lower than normal. I think he holds many grudges, that he cultivates the reputation of a dangerous person, and that having achieved this reputation makes him feel safe.

"Here is another incident that shows just how odd Catlanato's acts of revenge could be. A local judge told me that Catlanato had been brought before him as a kid. What had happened is this. Catlanato had a beef, a resentment, against a neighbor, a middle-aged man who was a psychiatrist, who was a snob, in the opinion of both Catlanato and the judge and who has snubbed young Catlanato. And you know Catlanato must strike back. So, he takes a whole gallon of red paint, blood red, and spills it on the street in right front of psychiatrist's driveway in an effort to scare him, which it did. But the kid was observed, so he came up before the judge who told me 'I listened to this kid and then I asked him 'Are you trying to tell me that this was an accident?' And he says 'Yes, your honor; thank you very much.' But he was grinning like a wise guy. 'Can you explain to me what you were doing with an open can of paint in the middle of the street and not even in front of your own house?' 'It's my hobby, your honor.' 'Hobby?' 'Yes, your honor. Some people collect stamps. I like to walk around carrying a can full of paint. I don't have your level of education, your honor, but I'm thinking that's not illegal. Am I right?' Catlanato was by now, beaming. The judge said. 'I'm going to find you guilty of vandalism and require you to pay the cost of restoring the pavement.'

"A somewhat different picture emerges for Richard Kuklinski, the Ice Man. You can go on line and see this revealed in his prison interview with the forensic psychiatrist Park Deitz. At the end of the interview, Deitz presents his diagnosis. Approximately one percent of the population has antisocial personality disorder and another one percent is clinically paranoid. Neither is particularly rare, but the combination is. Kuklinski has a violent father and, although that is not rare, the extent of the violence is. As an adolescent, Richard Kuklinski's older brother dies of injuries inflicted by their father and then he watches in silence as the family covers it up. His mother was also a violent woman, and again, that combination is rare. Now there is another part of his making that Deitz did not emphasize and that is his early experimentation with violence. Kuklinski was still in high school when the following incident happens. He's in a New Jersey bar, a place frequented by mafia types. A middle-aged man, a boss of some kind, shoves Kuklinski aside and calls him a stupid kid. This produces an absolutely astonishing degree of resentment in Kuklinski. He sits quietly, brooding and nursing a drink for the next couple of hours. Kuklinski leaves the bar and when he gets to his car, he notices the same mafia boss asleep in his own car, with the windows rolled down, as it was a hot night.

"Kuklinski has a can of gas in his trunk and very carefully, he places the gas can in the passenger seat beside the man who insulted him and he torches that car, killing its occupant. Imagine the reputation he gets. Other kids are bragging about winning fights or scoring with girls. This guy has killed a made-man. That's just a little different. There was also another incident, again when he was in high school, when Kuklinski gets in his car and just takes off aimlessly. All the way down in Georgia, he's on a country road when he gets cut off by a car full of five rednecks. They continue to follow Kuklinski, harassing him and shouting at him. He stops his car and they do the same. These guys have no idea of what they are dealing with. Kuklinski kills all five and he takes the opportunity of the interview to explain the circumstances behind this cold case. Kuklinski was also a six-foot five-inch bruiser, and this too adds to the perfect storm.

So that's it. That's my story. I think I may have missed out on the uplifting part after all. Hah-hah."

The Death of the Physician

The next morning, first light came slanting into the room from the small windows high above. The Gentleman was ladling the usual slop onto the captives' plates and behind him, stood another terrorist, rifle by his side. The Sergeant-at-Arms looked around at his sleepy comrades and noticed the Physician was not among them. He got up. "I'm going to see if I can rouse Ken. This slop won't be available for long. This ain't a hotel with continental breakfast."

A minute later he was back at the table, reporting "Holy shit! He's dead."

"Are you sure?"

"I touched his forehead. He's cold. That's a funny thing. If you touch a ham or a leg of lamb, say, and if it's room temperature, that's how you feel it. Normal. But if you touch a human being and they are room temperature, it feels like a block of ice. I've touched a dead guy before, but never one who was dead all night."

They all ran to Ken's bedside. Someone pulled back the blanket covering him. He wasn't a big man in life, but in death he looked to each of them so small and so fragile.

The Physiologist said "I'm going to miss Ken. He was an interesting man." All agreed.

Soon, the Gentleman was there, pressing the back of his hand to the forehead of the corpse. He stood up and smiled.

"You did this, asshole." shouted the Sergeant-at-Arms.

"What of it? I don't see the consequence, being that his family doesn't know."

"What's it got to do with his family?"

"We brought him out here at great expense to ourselves. Now, I think the family can pay his way home."

The Sergeant-at-Arm erupted. He ran and dove at the Gentleman Terrorist in an attempt to tackle him. However, the Gentleman reacted with lightning speed. His rifle was at his side and the muzzle was already pointing down. He set it firmly onto the floor and braced it with one foot. He went down on the other knee and bowed his head while grasping the rifle stock firmly with both hands. At the same time, he shouted 'Don't shoot' in his native language for the benefit of his confederate. The Sergeant-at-Arms landed on his chest against the butt of the rifle and rolled to the floor. He lay curled up in a ball in so much pain he could not speak.

The Gentleman snapped to attention with the rifle by his side. "You see, my friend, speed is better than size. That is something you Americans do not understand. You with your obsession with football and basketball."

After this incident, the captives sat down for their meal. Someone noticed that the Ski Bum was not among them. "This is the second time I've woken up and not seen him. Where is he? He's not in the bathroom." There was talk about the Ski Bum and how he had appeared so troubled. The Physician had been attempting to get him through withdrawal, coke was the common opinion. But what could he do without access to medications?

The First Engineer's Tale

After the captors had taken the body of the Physician away, the group sat down to their meal, which they ate in silence. When they were finished, Victor Forzley addressed the group. "I suppose it's my turn to tell a tale. This is the story of Raymond Woolrich, founder of the aerospace firm where I work, which is WTZ. That stands for Woolrich, Thompson and Zacharias. This is the story of how Woolrich got to be a very wealthy man while still in his twenties. Wealthy in a self-made kinda way; see he was born into money and he had all kinds of advantages in early in life. But to his credit, Raymond Woolrich knew how to use those advantages too. He had the gift of gab. They used to say he could sell hams in a synagogue. 'Gift of gab' is often another way of sayin' 'skilled manipulator; and Mr. Woolrich was that too. Even in his late seventies, which is when I knew him briefly, he still cut an impressive figure; tall, handsome, a voice that was deep and resonant, altogether an imposing presence.

"When I started at WTZ, Mr. Woolrich had already retired due to poor health, but he still gave company parties at his estate. I met him at one of those parties and we talked one-on-one for what had to be an hour. I think he liked me. He gave me his card and said 'Call and come back again. I have a story I'd like to tell you.'

"So, I came back and he told me the story of how WTZ was founded, a story that at one time was well enough known, but also one that he had kept under wraps in later years and had now become the subject of much rumor and speculation. I arrived at the big house that was set back fifty yards from the gate. That's a lot of land in L.A. County. A servant of answered the door. He told me 'Mr. Woolrich is expecting you.' and he led the way. I could hear the crack of billiard balls. I entered a wood-paneled room. Woolrich was lining up a shot.

On rolling tray beside him stood a bottle of single malt scotch, a bucket of ice and some glasses. He spent a little time asking me about myself. He said, 'I heard that you're a tennis player. I heard you played for USC on their championship team.'

"Not tryin' to brag, y'all. The point is that Mr. Woolrich does his homework."

"Shut the hell up, boy!" blurted the First Engineer's' friend Marcus, the Second Engineer. The First Engineer went on. "We played a few games of eight-ball, had a couple drinks. I can play a little and I quickly realized that I would have to tone down my game for the sake of the old man. As we played, Raymond Woolrich told me his story.

"In 1955, Mr. Woolrich was an aeronautical engineer working for McDonald Aircraft. He had several years of experience. The French government approached McDonald with the idea of producing military aircraft for them. Back in those says, Europeans did not speak English the way they do today. They needed a translator. Woolrich was way too junior to be a party to the negotiations, but he wrangled a role for himself as translator. Woolrich had a childhood that seemed custom-made to prepare him for the stunt he was about to pull. He had spent part of his youth living in France. He continued to study French in high school and college. He was fluent.

"The French party arrived in Southern California and there were only three of them; the Minister of the Armed Forces, a lawyer and a secretary. The Minister had the power to sign a deal if the right terms could be met. Even before they arrived, Woolrich had decided he would use his position as translator to tell the French that McDonald could not do the job. He would recommend to them another company. That company would be the little-known enterprise of Thompson Aircraft. Here's what he had in mind. Ross Thompson was his prep school friend and also a friend of the family. Ross's father owned the small firm of Thompson Aircraft. Their mutual friend Advil Zacharias would supply a large chunk of cash to kick-start the operation. Once the deal was signed, Woolrich would quit at McDonald and become a part of the new enterprise which would eventually be called WTZ, but not right away because the French could not know of his involvement. So, he was taking the job away from McDonald and giving it to himself. As he told me, he could not keep the smile from his face and he would break out in fits of laughter that would turn to fits of coughing.

"After some wining and dining, the French team and the McDonald team sat down for their first business meeting. The French wanted a lot. They wanted thirty-six bombers and two dozen jet fighters. This represented a major effort to get the French Airforce back on its feet after World War II. They presented a very ambitious set of specs including top speed, range, acceleration, payload and cost. McDonald engineers talked among themselves and agreed that the set of specifications was overly ambitious and presented some very real problems. Woolrich told me he was lucky and had to mistranslate only a little that first day. He told them that McDonald would need more time to assess the specs. Then Raymond Woolrich planted the first seeds of bad blood. He added that the demands were typically French. 'How do you mean that?' replied the affronted French Minister. Here, Woolrich responded, putting his words in the mouth of J. R. McDonald himself, 'If you knew a little more about aircraft, you might have done better against the Germans.' Then he told me that speaking purely as translator, he had offered a half-hearted apology for the remark. The mood turned dark and those on the McDonald side were mystified. Telling me this, the old man was doubled over, laughing and coughing. 'You must allow me my little indulgences.' he said. I had not seen this side of him before. He had always seemed such a figure of dignity.

"Cut to the chase, the second meeting did not go well either and Raymond Woolrich finally told the French that McDonald could not do the job. Those at McDonald thought the French were going home to await McDonald's counter-proposal. Instead, the French team stayed in California and signed with Thompson Aircraft. Woolrich had somehow managed to disguise the small size of the company and the job was completed with crews working around the clock. The rest is, as they say, history.

"By the time Woolrich had completed his story, he had lost three games of eight-ball in a row. Along the way, he had missed some very easy shots. He turned to me and said "Victor, I consider myself a pretty good pool player, what do you think?' When I hesitated a little, he said 'You don't think so, do you?' That made me a little uncomfortable and

I answered, 'I didn't say that.' He said, 'You didn't say it, but you think it.' I wondered why he was being so confrontational and so I said "OK, you could use a little practice.'

"He responded quickly 'A thousand dollars says I beat you in the next game. Make that a hundred. A hundred is more of a gentleman's bet.' I said 'OK, you're on.' And we both laid out a hundred on the tray. We lagged for break and I won. I sunk the seven on the break, so I had solids. Lucky seven. After that, I had no good shots, but instead of taking a defensive shot, I decided to try a very difficult shot to sink the three in the side pocket and I missed. That was my downfall. After that, Raymond Woolrich proceeded to sink all the stripes and then the eight. He looked up at me and smiled. God-damn if the old man wasn't hustling me! I said 'Alright, that was a hundred-dollar lesson. Mr. Woolrich, you still got it.' After that, we shook hands and I left. Raymond Woolrich passed away a couple of years ago.

"So that's my story. Marcus, my man, it's your turn."

Green Thomas

Marcus McCabe answered him "Victor, I don't know if I have a tale quite handy. Wait now, wait now. I *can* tell you a story that my Uncle Henry used to tell when I was a boy back in Virginia. Tall tale, really. Henry was my Daddy's older brother. At our family get-togethers, I used to help Uncle Henry at the grill. He would teach me how to cook and also tell me his Korean War stories. There were only two things wrong with that. First off, I never seen anyone get so many complaints over burnt hot dogs and burgers. Second, I later came to appreciate that soldiers who've seen real action; they don't talk about it the way Uncle Henry did. A walking tall tale; that's what he was.

"Uncle Henry loved to watch the outlandish things that he said sail right over my head. One time, he's telling me about the Battle of Chosin Reservoir. He said 'We come in over the frozen mud, with a couple of inches of snow on top. It cold, way up past the thirty-eighth parallel. Not a tree in sight. Trees illegal in Korea, boy. You grow a tree in Korea; they put yo ass in jail.'

"Because I was seven, maybe eight, I both believed him and didn't at the same time. Uncle Henry was one of those adults that gets a big kick out of the crazy things that kids will believe. But I'm not so sure they really do believe. Not exactly, anyway. What I think happens is that they know better, but their imagination overpowers them. Take the case of my sister Stella. She went up to stay with our cousins in New York. They had an oak dresser in the bedroom and in the wood grain, Stella could see the Big Bad Wolf and she was scared to death of it. That dresser is still in the family and I've seen it. You can definitely see the wolf's chin and the claws on one paw digging into the wood. But did my sister *actually* believe in the wolf? In this case, I can definitely say of course not. No one can believe that a wolf is inside a piece of wood. On top of that, there were no wolves for a very great distance. She was in New York City. To me, it's very clear that what scared her was not what she believed, but what she could imagine.

"It was the same with me when I listened to Uncle Henry. He said the Chosin Reservoir was shaped like an octopus, with six arms. Mama slapped him on the back and said, 'Henry an octopus has eight arms. Don't confuse the boy.' I asked him 'Uncle Henry, about that reservoir; who chosen it?' He laughed, like he did at all my questions. 'Who? What, boy? Who chosen what, now?' I asked him again 'The Chosin Reservoir, Uncle Henry; who chosen it and why was it chosen?' He lay back and laughed. He said 'Boy, you don't chosen no reservoir, the reservoir done chosen *you*. Done chosen lotta men that day.' He muttered that last part under his breath. The man was pleased with himself, alright.

"He told me how they served peas at mess every day and that what was left over went into the batch for the next day. Now, strictly by the laws of chance, some peas survived two or three or rarely even more meals. During this time, they went through a transformation, turning first hard, then yellow, then brown and finally black.

"But the stories I remember best were about a man in his company, a soldier they called Green Thomas. One time I asked Uncle Henry 'What kinda name is Green Thomas? It don't sound like any name I ever heard before.' Uncle Henry put me off like he always did. He said Green Thomas was the strongest man in the whole twenty-fourth infantry. He told me how Green Thomas could do hand clap push-ups."

"Sounds like bullshit, McCabe." interrupted the First Engineer. "Get down and give me five hand clap push-ups. Five is all I need. You can't *do* five; can't do *one*."

"I'm not even gonna to try, but I think y'all know what it is. You push up so hard that your hands leave the ground just long enough that you have time to clap them together before the next push-up. Well, I asked again how Green Thomas got his name and Uncle Henty put me off again. He told me how the Sarge asked him 'Hey Thomas, do you have a match?' to which the big man answered, 'Yeah, sure do.' and reached into his pocket. Sarge barked at him 'Thomas, you didn't address me as sir. Get down and give me fifty push-ups.' Green Thomas did the fifty push-ups, *hand-clap* push-ups. 'Now' Sarge asked him again 'Thomas, do you have a match?' Green Thomas stood tall, snapped to attention and told him 'Sir, no sir!'

"I said, 'I know, Uncle Henry, but Green Thomas still don't sound like a name to me.'"

"He said 'Alright, boy. Alright. I'll tell you how he got that name. It was the first day in boot camp. He come in lookin like a big city hipster with his putty-colored suit and a shaved part on each side of his head. I never heard no one use the word 'sir' more often, or mean it less.

"Now that same morning, we had a roll call. Green Thomas, he already sneaked him a look at the Sarge's clipboard. We was all listed first-name-first, all except Green Thomas. See, I was 'Henry McCabe' but he was 'Green, Thomas'; that's Green *comma* Thomas. It had to be some kinda mistake. I'm guessing it was copied off some other list where they put the last names first. See what I mean, boy?'

"I kinda nodded and Uncle Henry went on. 'Sarge, he called our names, one at a time. But when he called Thomas Green, didn't no one answer. He it called again. 'Thomas Green, front and center!'

"There was a big pause when nobody said nothing. Then Green Thomas took a step forward. 'The name is Green, Thomas sir.' Said it with a big old smirk on his face.

'Your name is not Thomas Green? It says Thomas Green here.' Sarge was a little slow on the uptake.

'Sir, I believe it says Green, Thomas. Thomas is my *last* name. You will notice that it is correctly alphabetized under T.'

"The sergeant didn't ask how he knew that. He just went on. 'It says Green *comma* Thomas. Are you tellin me your first name is Green *comma*.'

'The comma *is* a part of my name, sir, but it's silent. It is not pronounced.'

'How the hell do you pronounce a comma?'

'A comma is usually pronounced as a pause, sir. But here, there is no pause. One proceeds from Green, directly to Thomas as if one were describing Thomas, who is green. If you will allow me to wax metaphorical, I can tell you that the beginning of Green, Thomas is much like the beginning of green tomatoes. I say metaphorical because, as you may know, my people were planters; from the Old Country; South Carolina.'

'I don't like your style, Thomas.'

'Sir, if you're referring to my name, you'll have to take that up with my parents. They're the ones who named me, sir. Actually, you would need to speak with the parents of my grandfather. They started it all. You see, I'm proud to say that I'm Green, Thomas the fourth. They're both dead now, but I can put you in touch with a first-class medium.'

'Medium what?'

'Never mind that, sir.' He was smirking at the ground, as were a few others who shared his low opinion of the Sarge's intelligence.

'You're smiling, son and I don't see a damn thing to smile about.'

'Sir, it's just that I enjoy the repetition.'

'I don't follow you, Thomas.'

'What I enjoy, sir, is the ritual of explaining this. I'm forced to do it almost every day of my life and yet I've actually grown quite fond of it.' Well, from that day forward, we called him Green Thomas or sometimes just Tom. Today, Tom is a name on the wall. I don't have to tell you how they got it spelled it.'

"He told me how Green Thomas carried a wounded man five miles on his back. How he killed thirteen men in hand-to-hand combat. How he was the first man in the regiment killed. But another time he told me Green Thomas was sent home on a blue ticket.

'Blue ticket, what's that?' I asked. Henry gave me his usual kind of explanation, one that didn't explain a thing. He said 'The blue ticket was what they call a special designation for a man who served his country. *Was*, I say; they don't have it no more. The man with a blue ticket served his country; they can't say he didn't. But they don't want to say he served with honor, don't want to say it out loud because maybe the man had a little bit too much self-respect for their way of thinkin. Blue ticket. Ticket to the blues – that's what it was. You try getting a job with a thing like that on your record.'

"Uncle Henry also told me some stories that he says Green Thomas told him. How as a child he slept through the fire that killed his sister and cousin. But later he told Henry he had set the fire himself while playing with matches, that no one was hurt, that it plagued him to watch his aunt and uncle suffer the loss of their house and that Henry was the first person he had ever confided in. But another time yet, Green Thomas was the cousin, the one who had arrived for the summer from Chicago by train, just in time to witness the charred aftermath. These weren't exactly lies. Green Thomas, or more likely Henry, wished to inhabit the story from every perspective. He was like a ball player who went to sleep and relived the game in his dream. It was his aspiration to become a spectator and now, finally, he has done that."

"So, Green Thomas wasn't real, was he?" said the Psychologist.

"The part of Green Thomas that was real is that there was a little bit of *all* the men in him. And little bit of him remains to this day, though he's just a faint shadow and fading. But a least for now, he's still there, wherever you see smoke curling out of a cabin chimney, or a turpentine camp or a fish fry, or a backwoods sawmill or one of those little white churches with the blue or sometimes purple windows. Green Thomas is a souvenir, rescued from past. Take a look; he won't last long."

The Ski Bum and the Gentleman

After the Second Engineer was finished, the Sergeant-at-Arms went right back to his old routine. He bellowed "Where the hail is Hale? He must be with Pepe Le Pew again. Can't you just picture the two of them: 'Come to me to the Casbah, my little sweet potato. Zee cabbage does not run away from zee corned beef. It is love at first sight, is it not?'"

He went on "Hale and Frenchie are sweet, alright. I can almost hear those two love birds. Where are you, my little object of art? I am here to collect you. You know most men would be discouraged by now. But fortunately for you, Bebe, I am not most men."

Suddenly, the door at the far end of the room opened and the Ski Bum came strolling out, whistling and full of energy. The others could hear the door being locked and barred behind him.

The Sergeant-at-Arms may have run out of jokes. In any case, he did not try to hassle the Ski Bum, who was full of energy. He was pacing around the room, re-introducing himself to each of the other, working the crowd. After a while, the Ski Bum looked at his bed and began anxiously searching for something. His demeanor suddenly turned dark as he stood up and announced to all "Where the hell is my jacket?"

Someone answered, "wherever you left it."

"My jacket was here when I left. Who took it?"

The Physiologist answered again, "nobody took your jacket. Nobody wants your jacket."

"That's a five-hundred-dollar leather jacket."

"So what? I'm telling you, nobody wants your damn jacket."

The Ski Bum grabbed him by the shirt. "So, it's damn jacket now?

Guess what, dude? I think you took it."

"No one took your jacket. You're just paranoid. It' still wherever you left it."

"I'm going to search everyone's stuff until I find the bastard who thinks this is funny."

At that point, everyone moved in close to the Ski Bum and spoke to dissuade him and finally, he calmed down and just went off by himself.

Needless to say, none of the others liked the Ski Bum a whole lot.

The Physiologist's Second Tale

"In good weather, my boy scout troop would take backpacking trips as often as once a month. This was back in the mid-sixties. We started hiking in the Adirondack Mountains of upstate New York. Then we hit on a plan of hiking sections of the Appalachian Trial, which was a little closer to our home base in Connecticut. Each trip, we'd cover twenty miles or so and then on the next trip, pick up where we left off. We started in Vermont and eventually made it all the way to Pennsylvania.

"In August of 1967, we made one of those weekend trips in mid-state New York, with four or five fathers and twenty or so scouts, ranging in age from eleven to eighteen. At the end of the weekend, four of us older scouts stayed on to hike for another week on our own. Gene was straight-laced. He wore his full uniform the entire week and took the Boy Scout handbook with complete seriousness. Rick was popular and a little conflicted about still being in Boy Scouts. Dave was a fun-loving type. On the way home, the rest of the troop had driven through Woodstock, where Rick's Dad had left a car, so the four of us could drive home a week later.

"The trail was mostly through the woods but, at times, followed short stretches of two-lane blacktop. Along the trail, we argued the pros and cons of the Vietnam War, mainly because Gene was gung-ho for it and wouldn't let up. The other three of us were against it. Gene had a huge and heavy pack with every convenience of home. The rest of us packed lighter and had freeze-dried food; something new at the time. In our canteens, we had the traditional Boy Scout cocktail, made by taking the top quarter inch from every liquor bottle in your parent's cabinet. Combined with the metallic taste from the canteen, the mixture had a flavor that could be tolerated only by someone desperate to try adult vices. I remember the liquor cabinet in our house. Behind swinging doors, just above the opening to the crawl space was hidden a sparkling array of scotch, bourbon, vermouth, Drambuie, gin, Grand Marnier, you name it. My parents barely drank, but my Dad was in the construction business and gift bottles arrived every Christmas. Rick had a pack of menthol cigarettes which some of us shared.

"Kaaterskill Falls was memorable. We climbed the steep trail beside it. The falls had two stages and behind the lower falls was a hollowing out, a kind of a cave. There was a great, flat stone shelf behind the lower falls and it might have been fun to camp there for the night, except that it was too wet with mist. We swam in the pool blow the lower falls. The water was still very cold.

"Most nights, we stayed in lean-tos built during the Depression by the Civilian Conservation Corps. We had a couple of one-burner propane stoves for cooking, but we always wanted a campfire as well. For that, we would stop along the trail to collect strips of birch bark, because that makes the best kindling. We had matches, but we would always try first to light the campfire with flint and steel. Before going to bed, you would throw a rope over a tree limb and hoist your pack up out of the reach of bears. While gathering firewood, I found and arrow head. It was a thing of beauty, tan colored, glassy but slightly dull, perfect facets, probably chert. I still have it on my dresser.

"Toward the end of our trip, late in the afternoon on our second-to-last day, the trail broadened a bit. It was not until later that we realized that the trail had actually become a dirt road and was approachable by car from the opposite direction. We found a place to camp beside a stone wall and not far from the road. On the other side of the stone wall was an open field. We had just finished dinner and settled in early in the two pup tents that we had. It hadn't been dark for an hour, when we began to hear the roar of motorcycles, dozens of them.

"We were all steeped in the folklore surrounding motorcycle gangs. We had seen pictures of Hell's Angels in magazines, heard tales of rumbles in which people were knifed, how they had descended on a tiny town in Montana and had half destroyed the place, how they had tortured and murdered innocent people. Quickly, we collapsed the two tents. Clutching our hatchets to our chests, we moved, like inchworms in our sleeping bags, up close to the stone wall, thinking this was the best way not to be seen. Soon, the bikers had a fire going. We heard a lot of hoarse-voiced shouting. A guy sat down on the stone wall right above me. I could see he had on a motorcycle club vest, but I couldn't read it. He kept yelling 'fuckin-A' and I could hear his black laughter echoing through the trees. Later someone threw an entire can of gas into the fire and for a second or two, the explosion lit up the sky a dark and fiery orange and it looked like we were on the outskirts of Hell. Can you imagine? The flying metal could have cut someone in half. In the very early hours of the morning, it started raining and that broke up the party and we heard them all roar off. The morning light found us happily alone. They never saw us.

"We hiked a short distance into West Saugerties and had breakfast at a diner. Then we continued on to Woodstock. Woodstock already had a reputation as a capital of the counter culture, as they called it then. Bob Dylan lived there. We were all very curious. We walked through town and it was very quiet on a Tuesday morning.

"We continued outside of town and when we were out in the country we saw a dirt path that led into the woods and up a slight rise. At the end of the path we found an old wooden church crowded in among evergreens so closely that they nearly obscured it. The great door at the front of the church was locked, so we walked around it and inspected it from all sides. The church had once been white, but most of the paint had flaked off it. Still, it was so well-built that it could have easily been restored. There was a small house beside the church and a man answered the door in his bathrobe. He was in his sixties and he looked both distinguished and disheveled. "What can I do for you boys?" he asked. We took off our backpacks and stepped inside. He introduced himself as a pastor and he made us English muffins and hot tea.

"He was eager to show us the church. He may have been a pastor, but from the looks of the church, it was obvious there was no congregation. The floor was dusty and dirty and the pews were in disarray. The pastor wore a white robe. He was stooped. He had thick and lanky hair that was somewhere between white and tan and was also a little dirty. Under the robe, he wore white pants that were too long and were rolled up at the bottom. The bottoms of his pants dragged on the ground behind his heels and were wet. Rick later called him 'Swamp Shoes'. The pastor probably had not had any human contact in a while and so the occasion of meeting us unleashed a word torrent.

"He was most anxious to tell us about medieval art and the old books that he had. Some paintings were hung around the main room of the church. In a room behind the altar were more paintings stacked along the walls and a table covered in books. He opened a bible from the fifteen-hundreds. He described the paintings and books in great detail, but as this happened fifty years ago, the details are a little hazy in my mind. I remember a painting on three panels. The center panel was a nativity with a lot of blues and dark colors, the shallow perspective like a Giotto and the occasional use of gold. There was a large painting in somber blues and greys of soldiers lining a battlement.

"When asked where he had gotten all these things, the pastor was vague. "I've been a collector all my life." That hardly answered the question. If these artifacts were really what they seemed to be, they were worth a great fortune. What were they doing in a dank and musty place that would speed their deterioration and where no one could see them? To this day, I think they may have been ill-gotten loot from World War II.

"At the time, my Dad had recently been the Project Manager for the construction of the Beinecke Rare Book Library at Yale University. After completion of the library, he had taken a position at Yale as the Buildings and Grounds Officer. He was most interested in my story. He was at first a little incredulous, but he was won over by my ability to describe the scene in vivid detail. He contacted officials at the university who went up to Woodstock and meet the pastor. I heard that on the second trip, they convinced him to donate the books so that they could be properly preserved. The rarest of books were kept under helium and I imagine that some of the books from Woodstock qualified for that privilege. I don't know what happened to the paintings. Funny, I never did learn much about the identity, the validity or the value of the books. You'd think that some official might invite me to his office and explain those things. After all, I was directly responsible for bringing a treasure to them. But that's the way things were back then. Kids were to be seen and not heard. So, no one paid any attention to my contribution."

The Bartender's Tale

Elytra was wearing her uniform from The Tubes, tuxedo shirt with black slacks. Her silky black hair had two perfect streaks, one green and one magenta. Her head was tilted slightly to one side as she spoke.

"Before I begin, it seems like we have another listener. Look at this visitor from outer space." On the table, stood an amazing insect. Supported on long skinny legs, it had a body like a square-cut jewel. It was so reflective and had so many facets, that it was impossible to tell its real color. Its little red eyes rotated on stalks. The insect stood in a sliver of sunlight that made a perfect spot light for it to shine in. It stood tall and proud and swayed with two different rhythms.

"Isn't he beautiful?" Elytra went on. "He looks alien to us, but to him *this environment* must be alien. There are no trees in here, it doesn't rain and his life can be ended at any moment by a rolled-up newspaper."

"His life is like ours." snapped the Sergeant-at-Arms. "One, we have no idea where this hell hole is located on the face of the globe. Two, if these bastards ever find out they can't get any money out of us, well, that's your rolled-up newspaper right there."

"Speaking of amazing insects, do you remember the moth?" asked the Psychologist.

"How could I forget it?' said Elytra. "It had wings the size of my two hands, side by side."

"That's right, you saw it fly away right after I touched it. It was on a pole and I touched it by mistake, without realizing it was there. It was like a feathery green cape, draped over broad shoulders. A current of electricity ran through me when I realized I had touched it."

Elytra began her tale. "My story is set in another place of fabulous insects; Iquitos Peru, in the Western Amazon. Chris found an ad in the back of Weed Magazine for a tour that included back-packing, a boat ride and an ayahuasca ceremony. Do you know what that is?"

After receiving some blank stares, she explained. "Ayahuasca is a drug ceremony of cleansing and enlightenment. It's been practiced in the Amazon basin for thousands of years. Four of us decided to go; Chris and I, Richard and Gloria. Getting there was difficult and expensive. We had to fly in over the Andes. Iquitos is a frontier city, a Wild West town, full of bordellos and saloons, livestock for sale in the street, curio shops with native art and oddities like python skins. At Iquitos, the smooth clear water of the Itaya meets the lurching tan water of the Amazon.

"We were in a bar, drinking shots of pisco, and that's where we met Nolan, another American. Nolan was spending the entire winter in the Amazon. He and his two companions, one a local guide, had just been to Angel Falls in Venezuela. He told us they had flown into Kamarata and along the way, got their best view of the Falls from the air. They crossed rainforest and savannah and clear streams to reach the base of Auyan Tepui, a nine thousand-foot-tall escarpment of pink and black sandstone. It is possible to scale the rock face, but instead they took a steep trail, up past the statue of Simon Bolivar, to the top of the tepui. They explored the immense table land that collects the water for the falls and then Nolan and his friend parachuted to the bottom, while their guide went back down the trail. 'Did you parachute near the falls?' one of us asked. 'Hell no, you stay the fuck away from the falls.' answered Nolan. 'The falling water creates down-currents of air that can drive you down, or worse yet, collapse your parachute.' Nolan decided to join us for the ayahuasca ceremony the next day.

"The next morning, we met outside a green building with a corrugated roof. There were about two dozen of us and we were separated into two groups. Gloria and I were in the first group. The three men were in the second. Our group was seated in a darkened room. Don Luis was to be our guide. He blessed each of us and gave us oil to rub on our bodies for protection. He blew tobacco smoke over our heads. We were each given a cup of ayahuasca, which we had to drink straight down. It was greenish brown, bitter and hard to swallow.

"After a short while, we moved into the next room where we sat in the dark and silence, waiting for the effects to start. In those days, Gloria was a wild one. I don't know where she is today. Just to give you one example, she and Richard had a very open relationship, lots of partners. I remember a party in Connecticut on about five acres of woods. There was a pond covered with lily pads and they were in flower; beautiful. We all set up our picnic on one side of the pond and on the far side you could clearly see Gloria and some guy on a blanket going at it. Richard was telling anyone who would listen. 'That's my wife out there balling that dude.' His excessive pride gave me the creeps; still does. What are you hiding, Richard? I never did trust him. To make things worse, Richard and Gloria had baked a banana bread that was full of marijuana and left it on the table without telling anyone. Michele and Suzie ate most of it without knowing what was in it and soon, they were on another planet, scared, but angry too. Richard just continued to insist that it was cool. The two of them ended up leaving early and going on a boat tour of the Thimble Islands to come down from their high.

"After sitting in the dark room for ten minutes, I felt tingling and burning and nauseous. I threw up into the bucket I was given. Most of us did. I could hear the sounds of wind and rushing water. My jaw felt numb. I could hear Chris's voice in the other room. He said, 'This shit smells like shoe polish.' His voice was so tiny and far away. I felt embarrassed and then a moment later, I felt foolish for having been embarrassed. Gloria was right beside me, but the visions had started and I couldn't see her. We often say, 'I can just picture that.' But with a vision, it's not just a figure of speech, you can literally picture things, and picture them so strongly that it overpowers your ability to see what is *actually* there. I was searching for Gloria's face and I found it in a grass mat, hanging on the wall. There were little windmills behind her and I guess that was because she is blonde and mostly of Dutch background. I looked at Gloria's face and she seemed to be telling me that she loved me, that she would always be there for me. She really was a doll, despite the weirdness.

"Suddenly, I found myself walking down a slowly turning tunnel of branches, walking toward the light. But it wasn't the 'light at the end of the tunnel' effect that people sometimes refer to, a light that is far away and small. Instead, I was almost there, almost in the light.

With just another step, I would be bathed in it. But there I stayed, in a suspended state of almost becoming. How long? It seemed like both an instant and an eternity. I was beginning to fill up with light. It was pouring out of my eyes. I looked at Don Luis and the edges of his face were turning gold.

"Outside the tunnel, in the light, was a clearing in the jungle, and we were all seated around a circle of packed earth. I heard drumming, there were lots of drums, and above it a thin ribbon of music played on a pipe. Into the circle came a line of African dancers. One wore a tall pointed head piece covered in cowrie shells. He had on an ebony mask with slit eyes and tin teeth filed to a point. He wore a striped tunic and a raffia skirt. One wore a costume that looked like a shaggy fur with hundreds of pieces of brown cloth sewn on that shook with every step. The fur was pink around his collar and he wore a white and brown antelope mask. Next, a ghostly, high-stepping figure in black and white. He had a white face and attached to the top of his head was something like a many-legged stool placed upside down. They danced and they stomped and they raised the dust. I had seen them all before in a museum video. Then came the figure who was clearly the boss. He wore a suit of green leaves that shook as he stamped furiously and menacingly to the relentless drums. He wore a fish mask with long ropes coming from its upper edge. He danced by alternating his feet in the same spot. He twisted violently and shook his leaves. He stood with his legs apart and flailed his mane against the dirt. He chased the other dancers from the ring. He charged at me, causing me to retreat back into the tunnel. He charged at the drummer and at the piper. Then he lay down and writhed in the dirt until, at last he was still. The drummer straddled him and the piper came back and played quietly until the dancer came back to life. Then he charged at me again. But this time, I was not frightened. I knew it was Don Luis inside the costume and I could see every molecule in the air between us. I knew also that he wasn't threatening me; he was challenging me. With that, I stepped out into the light and he was gone.

"Finally, we moved into a shady garden. They brought glasses of iced tea for us to sip on as the effects of the ayahuasca began to wear off. I saw the face of my father filling the sky, a father whom I have only met a few times in my life. The image of his face was faint and made of blue and copper-colored clouds. How did he find me, all the way down there? I don't even know where he is. His body is in Rutledge Cemetery in Chillicothe, Ohio. He said to me 'Elytra, I have been watching you. An I am proud that you are a happy person, despite being born out of sad circumstances.' I have always tried to hold on to that view of myself. Then the clouds moved and I lost him."

Higher and Sunnier

The Physiologist did not hear the Bartender's story. Once again, he was eavesdropping on Hi and Sunny as they sat together on the edge of a mattress.

Hi said "I wrote a little ditty for you." And he began to sing while strumming an air guitar.

"I dreamed we sailed to heaven
In a leaky kitchen drawer
And I dreamed we strolled together
Along God's golden shore

"But I opened my eyes this morning
To a world that's so unkind
One thing's still for certain
You're lookin' good, Miss Fine

"When you get that sinking feeling
That this nightmare might be real
Intelligent tapeworms of Pluto
They know how you feel

So, I called Mr. Myxomycetes
He's the Exchequer of the Pugh
He said I'd sure like to help you, son
But there's nothing I can do"

"That's all I've got, so far." he said. "How do you like it?"

"Intelligent tapeworms from Pluto." she laughed. "What is that?"

"I was in a bathroom stall one time. It was painted in a sloppy way and there were drips running down the wall. A bit of graffiti said 'Help! We're intelligent tapeworms of Pluto trapped between the layers of paint'. It kind of stayed with me."

"And Mr. Myxomycetes, that's not a real name."

"It's the scientific name for slime mold."

"That's a handy thing to know. Anyway, I like it; I like the idea. But you won't get any awards for your voice."

"Not to change the subject, but don't you think we should have the ceremony at Mount Lasser this summer?"

"We could take our vows while ski jumping side by side, you on water and me on snow."

"It would be a first; it would definitely be a first."

The Physiologist continued listening, well-pleased with what appeared to be a strong relationship forming.

The Lawyer's Tale

The eleventh morning, the captives awoke to a storm. It had been storming all night. Hard rain was drumming down on the roof. It was dark; the mood was almost that of night-time. Flashes of light came in through the high windows.

The Lawyer spoke up. "Maybe it's time for me to tell a story. This is about Jose. He was my older brother and if you really want to know the truth, he was kind of a fuck-up. Hey, listen, I'm telling you that because I cared about my brother. He wasn't a *bad* dude. In fact, his downfall was that he got himself into a situation that he was too soft-hearted to deal with. You'll see.

"After high school, he spent a long time in a nothing job. I used to tell him 'What are you doing to yourself, Jose? You work in that furniture refinishing place and you breathe the paint stripper and lacquer all day because they have no ventilation and then you drink every night at those clubs in Venice. You are poisoning yourself, night and day. And you are not saving a penny. You have no plans for the future. I have to tell you this because I care about you.' And I did. I did. You know Jose was a smart kid and he played the guitar so well. He was always good to our mother.

"So, here's the story. One night, Jose and his amigos are drinking in a club. I think it was called The Slam Dunk. The whole evening, everyone is asking where's Angel, where's Angel? A band was playing loud and it was hard to talk. When they get ready to leave, they find him on the sidewalk outside the club, sitting against the front wall. It seems like he is too drunk to move on his own, so they pack him into the car. Juan and Romauldo, who were Angel's roommates, carry him inside the apartment and put him into his bed. In the morning, they discover he is dead, shot three times. The cops had a hard time

"

believing this story. They said yes, we heard the part where you said you were drunk, but your friend was dead, how do you not see that? Well, he was wearing a dark jacket and they didn't see the blood. I represented Jose and his friends; not in court (they were never charged). I represented them during questioning and eventually they were cleared of wrongdoing.

"Soon after that, Jose decided he wanted to make more money the easy way, so he got in with the Avenidas. Bad idea. Okay, I know what you are going to say. They are a drug gang, but don't the Knuckle Draggers make and sell meth, so who am I to talk? First, yes, the Knuckle Draggers do sell meth. I can say that because Arnie has already told you. But I am okay because I'm a lawyer, because I'm not selling any drugs and because I know how to take care of myself. Arnie is okay because he has money and legal protection. But some of the guys under Arnie; that's a different story. Sometimes bad things happen to them. I didn't want that for Jose. Plus, Jose did not know how to take care of himself. He was a guy who wouldn't hurt a flea; so, what was he doing there?

"It was only a matter of time before something happened. Jose was delivering a shipment. His car was boxed in and he was robbed. That night, he came to me and he said, 'Dolores, I'm in big trouble.' In the morning, we went to the bank and I gave him ten thousand dollars. Then he needed to be on his way to Mexico, to San Francisco, Guanajuato, to go into hiding with his childhood friend who they call Tomatillo. He didn't tell me that, but I knew.

"San Francisco is the city in Mexico where Jose and I were born. It is a city of beautiful colonial buildings. Too bad there are no jobs there. For over a century, the silver mines of San Francisco del Rincon were the richest in the world. Each mine had its own cathedral. When the silver ran out, the tramways and tunnels of the mines became the streets of the city. Today, the sunken streets and tunnels are a tourist attraction. Some of the tunnels are narrow and have rough walls of rock. Others are spacious and have vaulted ceilings of brick or stone. There is also the Callejon de Beso, the Alley of Kisses. This is where the balconies on the two sides almost meet in the middle. It is said that a very wealthy man forbade his daughter to see a young man of poor background. The boy arranged for access to the apartment across the street and they were able to kiss across the balconies. Our family moved from San Francisco del Rincon to L.A. when I was ten and Jose was thirteen. I haven't been back since.

"Just a couple of days after Jose left, I received an unwelcome visit from a representative of the Nuestra family. Do you know that asshole blew by the receptionist and stormed right into my office? He demanded to know where Jose might be. I told him 'You're not going to get anything from me. But you shouldn't have to ask. Don't you know anything about your own people? What kind of half-assed operation do you run?' He said, 'You better not fuck with us or it could turn out badly for you and your family.' I said, 'Did you know the threat that you just made has been recorded?' Then he grabbed me and said, 'Illegal recording don't count for nothing.' I told him 'Hey stupid, it's not me recording you, it's the cops and they already have it. You could go to jail for what you just said. Did you forget you're dealing with a lawyer?'

"Then he asked me 'Do you know my name? I don't think we have been introduced.' I had to admit to myself that I didn't. Then I told him I didn't want to press charges., that I wanted a solution to the situation. I told him Jose didn't cheat them; he was robbed of the dope on his way. The man answered 'Now who's being naïve, senora? Jose has a debt to pay. He can pay it with the dope, four hundred thousand dollars or his life. We are flexible that way.' I wish to God I could have smacked the smirk off his face.

"Jose spent a couple of weeks in hiding with Tomatillo. Then came late October and the Day of the Dead. Jose was bored sitting inside all day. Tomatillo had a band and they were going to play on the sidewalk in one of the tunnels. Jose wanted to play guitar with them. He always loved the Day of the Dead ceremony and San Francisco del Rincon has one of the best. Tomatillo thought it was a bad idea. He told him, 'Jose, you are six-foot four. You are easy to spot.' But Jose pleaded with him and so he went out onto the street with them.

"That night was a big party on the streets of the city. There were thousands dressed like the dead with their faces painted or else wearing masks. Festival lights were strung everywhere. There were tables with arrangements of candles and orange marigolds. Tequila flowed. Fireworks filled the sky. That night, there were also many representations of Santa Muerta on the street. Some were kindly and offered prayers to all who passed. One exuded such an aura of malice that she was given a wide berth by all as she passed through the crowds. She was tall and she carried a scythe. Her black dress swept along the ground. She wore a calacas skull mask and a wreath of roses. She had a stiff-legged gait that did not look entirely female.

"Santa Muerta, the bad one, came to watch Tomatillo and his mariachi as they played on the sidewalk beside the traffic rushing through the tunnel. She stayed a short while, studying the small crowd and watching the band before moving on. The band played for several hours. They threw themselves into the music, but no one could say they really enjoyed themselves. An atmosphere of gloom and dread hung over the scene. By midnight, the beer, the tequila and the exhaust fumes were catching up with them. A couple of the musicians felt a little queasy.

"The figure of Santa Muerta returned. She watched the musicians for a long time. The general feeling of dread grew and, slowly the crowd began to thin out. Then, without warning, she pulled out a pistol, shot Jose twice through the guitar and disappeared into the night. And that is the story of my dear brother, the unfortunate Jose."

"How do you know these details of what happened on the street in Mexico?" Asked the Physiologist.

"Tomatillo came to the funeral in L.A. and he told me. And one last thing I'd like to add; a lesson for life. Always know where you belong and, most importantly, where you don't."

One by one, the other captives tried to comfort the Lawyer in her sorrow, which all could see was still fresh.

Click to Enlarge

Last to speak was the Programmer. As he stood to begin, a drum roll of muffled thunder could be heard in the distance.

"It's starting again, so early in the day. Said Lauren Campbell.

What I hate about these storms" said the Psychologist "is that I keep expecting them to relieve the humidity and they don't. Where I come from, it's cooler and dryer after a thunderstorm and here that doesn't happen."

"I'm a software developer. Early in my career, I worked for an online retailer and one of my assignments was to work on the part of the website that allows the viewer to enlarge the picture of each piece of merchandise and to rotate it in space. In theory, that is not such a hard job. But consider that this was a major company and that there may be literally thousands of people using the site at the exact same time. Rapid, flawless and simultaneous execution; there's the hard part. I enjoyed this assignment because it represented in a way, my theory that there is value in seeing life from the ant's perspective; that seen up close, the subtlety of events becomes apparent. Great mystery may be observed in the smallest things. That mystery is a secret, hidden in plain sight. I call my tale 'Click to Enlarge'.

"This is a story of a young man named John who was born into relative comfort and the bosom of the Catholic Church. I'm not sure if it has a moral per se, but I think the story at least raises questions. Still, I doubt that everyone will see the *same* questions. That's why I'm going to ask for some discussion after I tell the story. Now, before I begin the main part of the story, I want to give you a little background on John.

"On Friday afternoons, the Catholic kids were let out of Elementary School early for religious instruction. They would gather behind the

"

school to be marched single file a hundred yards or so to the Community Center. There they would recite the catechism and receive instruction from Sister Mary Ellen on the nature of sin, both venial and mortal. John spent a lot of time trying to decide in which category his greatest desires lay. His weekly Confessions would begin "Bless me Father, for I have sinned. I have had impure thoughts…" ten times, twenty times, continuously.

"One day, Sister Mary Ellen laid down an additional row of barbed wire for the children to negotiate. She told them that every time we commit a sin, it produces a black spot on our soul and when that sin is forgiven in Confession, the black spot is not entirely erased. Instead, she warned them, there remains a faint gray spot in its place. And when we are in heaven, as she was quick to add that she sincerely hoped they all would be one day, when the celestial light is shining through us all, the others will be able to see that faint gray spot and to know at once that we are a former sinner. At this point, Bobby Mullins jumped out of his seat, stood in the aisle and pointed directly at the nun. He told her 'When I die, baby, I want to *go* to hell. That's where all the swingers are!' Bobby was taken into another room where he was forced to lay his hands flat on the desktop while they were beaten with a yard stick. This scene made a strong impression on John.

"On days other than Friday, he would walk part of the way home from school with Mark Koehler, who was discovering the forbidden thrill of bad language. John would walk around the edge of the swamp, poking a stick in the mud and thinking to himself 'fuck this' or 'fuck that'. But he lacked the nerve to say it out loud because that was a venial sin and, although he went to Confession regularly, he was deathly afraid of that little gray spot. Mark, however, wasn't. In fact, he was barely capable of completing a sentence without a curse word and he could use the word 'fuck' as all seven parts of speech, the same ones they had all just learned them in class. Sometimes on the walk home, John would interview Mark, all the while dragging a stick along the stone wall that separated them from a little farm and always being careful never to let that stick lose contact with the wall. That farm had a few cows and sheep and maybe a couple of acres of vegetables. The interviews would go something like this. John would hold out a pretend microphone and ask 'Mark, the people out there in TV land want to know; what's your favorite word?' Mark would stroke his chin thoughtfully before answering 'Well gee, let me think for a fuckin second. You know what, why not just come the fuck out and fuckin say it? My favorite fuckin word happens to be fuck. Why the fuck not?' Then John would wrap it up for the audience. 'Well, there you have it, ladies and gentlemen, the Mark Kohler statement.'

"Up to the age of ten, this boy had never missed Mass, not even once. That first happened when the family was on vacation at a lake in upstate New York. The only road in or out ran along a valley between two steep hills. A Saturday night rainstorm had caused a small landslide that left three feet of earth and stone lying across the road. That Sunday morning, he and his father had dug until noon before it was declared a hopeless cause.

"Around the age of thirteen, John announced at the dinner table that he no longer wanted to be a priest. The funny thing was he could not remember ever having freely said that he wanted to be one in the first place. But over the years, he had found himself in countless conversations that started with 'later, when you are a priest…'.

"By high school, he had become a deist; that is, he believed in a God that placed His eye, but not His hand into the world. To put the matter another way, if asked, he would begin by saying that he believed in God, but if pushed hard enough, he would admit that he didn't know. To those who found that stance contradictory, he would ask since when does the value of story reside in its literal truth? He said that he didn't know, not that he didn't believe. And the reason for that difference is something that he had worked out carefully in his mind. Regarding the possibility of a next world, we know nothing and can know nothing. But stating that God does not place His hand into the world is tantamount to saying that we have no evidence for the existence of God. And on top of that, we never will. To propose a God who places His Hand into the world is to propose an unjust God. To propose that God answers the prayers of people with small problems is to propose that He does not care about people with big problems, problems that are not even remotely of their own making, but which are instead entirely foisted upon them. To propose that God answers prayers at all is to propose that He doesn't know what to do until we tell Him. So why not just come out and say that there is no God? We don't know if there is another world because we don't know if matter and energy is all there is to the universe. It is not necessary to propose that consciousness exists in order for the laws of physics to operate. Yet we know consciousness exists. More specifically, I know that I am conscious and by extension I assume that others are as well. We don't know what causes consciousness and it is sheer pretention on the part of neuroscientists who say that we are close to understanding it. We will never know; it is unknowable. However, that fact of consciousness creates the possibility that something survives death. A possibility; that is all. We will never prove or disprove it."

By now, the drum roll of thunder was more like a clash of cymbals. The room had darkened by degrees until it seemed like it must be twilight outside. The captives could not see outside, but instead received a little light only through some windows overhead. Rain beat down on the metal roof and from time to time, they could hear curtains of rain as they were blown against the side of the building. At times, it was difficult to hear The Programmer, but if his words were muffled, their dark import was amplified. The Programmer was entering the part of his story that was difficult to tell, the part that expressed underlying hostility.

He raised his voice a bit and continued, "Now, on to the main part of the story. As an adult, John moved his young family into their first home. He was hard working and kind. His biggest fault was that he took slights and insults too seriously. It was in those first years in the house that he learned, through two incidents, that a great power had been granted to him.

"The first incident that demonstrated this power involved his next-door neighbor who was also named John. So, I'll just refer to the neighbor as the psychiatrist. The neighbor was a somewhat older man, shy, insecure, and very snobby. The psychiatrist was skilled at implying a sense of his own superiority without your ever being able to say exactly how he did it. So, it was difficult if not impossible to catch him in the act. The young man grew increasingly sick of these insinuations and frustrated with his inability to confront his neighbor.

"After receiving yet another insult to his intelligence, John was fuming. He was quite confident that he was in fact smarter than the psychiatrist, and fantasized about having the chance to say so. John developed what can only be described as an unsavory habit. Each morning as he left for work, he would take a Q-tip with him and finish the job of cleaning his ear while starting the car. Then, as he sped away, he would flick the dirty Q-tip into the psychiatrist's yard. John's wife found out about this habit and was disgusted. John argued that there was little chance that the Q-tips would ever be found as the neighbor's yard was overgrown and looked like a place where a hermit might live. Despite this, the psychiatrist was excessively proud of his yard because it identified him a "Friend of the Earth". He wasn't fertilizing or wasting water. And he made it clear that he disapproved of John's well-cared-for lawn and plantings, which he saw as the mark of an unenlightened person, a conformist. He even went so far as to sneak into John's yard and turn off the water when he was watering the grass on other than a designated day.

"The psychiatrist had a cherry tree in his front yard, of which he was quite proud. Since the tree produced more fruit than he and his wife could use, he would give out little bags of the sweet dark cherries to others in the neighborhood. These cherries were dispensed with the largesse of a lord. The neighbor had a way of insinuating that he was giving you the most precious gift imaginable and that you should be eternally thankful. In doing so, he affected a collegial and gregarious air. John was working in his yard when he heard the psychiatrist pontificating. The joviality irritated him because the psychiatrist was not an outgoing person, but a very clear example of an introvert. John remembered the last insult he had received from the psychiatrist. Then he looked at the cherry tree and with all his heart, he wished it dead.

"At that moment, he felt a wave pass over him. His wasn't sure exactly what had happened and he was troubled by the uncertainty. The next morning, the cherries were all on the ground, rancid and inedible. The leaves had turned brown and would soon fall off. With a mixture of satisfaction and apprehension, he watched his neighbor tend to the tree, puzzle as to what was wrong. Within a week the tree was clearly dead and the psychiatrist cut it down. The young man was shocked by the power of what he had done. He now knew that a power had been granted to him and he was somewhat ashamed that he used that power in such a petty way. He resolved to use his power only for a higher purpose.

"The young man took stock in his secret power and as a result grew more confident. But sometimes he questioned whether that power was real. Could it have been merely a coincidence that the tree had died? Over a year passed before another incident occurred, one which eliminated all doubt. There was an enormous snow storm that lasted all day and all night. In the morning, the snow lay so deep that the smallest compact cars were completely obscured and full-sized cars were represented only by a small bump in the snow that lay chest-high. John and his wife had two cars. They kept one in the driveway and one on the street. Their street had alternate-side-of-the street parking and so it was necessary to move his car to the other side of the street, a daunting task. Dutifully, John got up early and set to work shoveling snow and clearing a path to the other side of the street. It took him until noon. In the late afternoon, the city snow plow came to clear the street. His was the only car that had been moved. Instead of towing all the other cars that were now on the wrong side of the street, city workers decided to tow John's car instead. John was outraged and decided to fight his ticket in court. The judge turned out to be an arrogant man, who not only ruled against John, but made it clear that he considered him foolish. The young man stood up and protested "That is unfair. I obeyed the law and I am being punished." The judge thundered "Sit down right now or I will hold you in contempt of court." Suddenly, the young man felt charged with impulse and he told the judge "You are jealous of me; jealous because I am an honest man and you are not." At this moment, the courtroom was filled with a sense of unreality. The young man could scarcely believe what he had just said. The judge responded with great anger. "Have it your way. I hereby sentence…". But he had only barely begun speaking when his voice started to trail away. The judge looked down in horror; his hands were turning green. He looked at his reflection in the glass beside the jury box and he saw that his face was also a bright and hideous green. A gasp ran through the small crowd in the courtroom. The courtroom was filled with the most intense and uncanny green and yellow light. It was as if a giant emerald were illuminating the room and turning slowly like a disco ball. The judge slumped over in his chair. Feebly, he banged his gavel and pronounced

"Case dismissed". The courtroom was cleared on account of fear.

"John walked out of the courtroom with a small victory, but truly he was shaken by this experience and he vowed never to use his power again, no matter what the circumstances. This time there could be no question that something had actually happened. As if to underscore that reality, he learned that the judge had suffered a minor stroke, from which he recovered, but remained weakened on one side.

"At this point, John's story becomes a little anti-climactic. He put away his secret power and with it the desires that might make one tempted to use it. As a result, he prospered. Without being so obsessed with slights, both real and imagined, John managed to receive his fair share of breaks. He had a career that could be described as moderately successful. It was not until late middle age that John was diagnosed with cancer and his resolve was again tested. Chemotherapy brought nausea and vomiting, entire days spent in bed. He knew he could abolish all this, but he didn't and eventually he passed into healthy remission. Now we have arrived at the Click to Enlarge moment. What I mean by that is ordinary lives, when examined up close, often contain extra-ordinary elements. When we learn of such things, we encounter mystery, we encounter things we never could have imagined."

As the story ended, the noise overhead and all around suddenly stopped and the sun was rekindled in the windows above. A lighter mood was restored, although the air was still oppressive."

"Your story says something a little different to me." put in the Psychologist. "It says that wishes that cannot be fulfilled, wishes that should not be fulfilled; those wishes are a burden."

"Yes, John was not only happier, but more successful, once he got rid of that burden." added Laurel Campbell.

The Programmer was pleased that his story had illustrated the value of self-control and the group was in general pleased to hear a story with a satisfying moral. A bit weird, but it wasn't meant to be taken literally, was it?

Operation Lily Pad

Operation Haystack had been a success. The American reconnaissance team had received a signal, a single ping, from a point near the shore of the island of East Timor, an island so far to the East that it was just off the coast of tropical Northwestern Australia. The team did not want to re-fly the route in order to confirm the ping. That could have caused them to be detected.

The success of the operation came quickly, so quickly that the planning for the next stage was not yet complete. A meeting was in progress in the White House Situation Room with the Australians present through secure video conferencing. Admiral Butterfield was standing in front of a lighted map of the South Pacific when the news location of the hostages arrived. He placed his finger on a spot in the Timor Sea and declared "I want a lily pad right here."

By good fortune, the location of the hostages on East Timor was only a hundred and fifty miles from Darwin RAAF Airbase in the far north of Australia. Final decisions could now be made as to exactly how the raid to free them would be carried out. Time was of the essence. If the reconnaissance planes had been spotted, this would mean that the terrorists might move the hostages, or worse. During the ensuing discussions, a plan quickly fell into place. There was a US Navy Seal team based out of Darwin RAAF Airbase. Quickly, the Australian Prime Minister gave his approval for a joint venture. The lily pad would be the Australian amphibious helicopter dock the HMAS Adelaide, which could deploy six attack helicopters or four transport helicopters and close to a thousand troops in case the operation required a land invasion. The Adelaide could make twenty knots and reach its destination in only five hours. The nearest American equivalent was nearly two thousand miles away in Guam; too far.

US Navy SEAL Team Six was already stationed in Darwin, deployed from Virginia Beach. The Australians would supply the staging site at Darwin RAAF, the Adelaide and her crew. The SEALs would conduct the rest of the rescue operation. The Adelaide would not carry assault troops. Instead, the US would deploy troops by transport ship from Guam and would be expected to arrive for a possible back-up role midway through the rescue operation.

Among those on the other end of the connection was Australian Admiral "Fill 'Er Up" Jack Randolph, so called because of his fondness for American bourbon. He sat in his favorite stuffed arm chair, taking occasional nips from a bottle he kept on the floor. He would be in charge of the plan to equip the Adelaide and have her cruise under cover of darkness, the very next night, to a spot just fifty miles offshore from the target on East Timor. Time was pressing, so much so that instructions were relayed and preparations begun even while the conference was still going on. On the American side, Admiral Colin Pitts, Naval Special Warfare Commander, began planning the raid with SEAL Team 6 leader Commander G. William Orange.

The Death of the Navy Pilot

Confederates of the terrorists had spotted American reconnaissance planes in the sky and had noticed their grid-like flight patterns. As a result, the terrorists were now aware of the possible presence of a tracking device among their captives. That afternoon, no meal was served. The captors appeared to be in a state of confusion. They could be heard could shouting behind the locked doors at the far end of the bunker.

In the late afternoon, the captives heard the main door unbolted and out came the Gentlemen with all six confederates by his side. All except the Gentleman himself were pointing pistols or rifles at the captives. The Gentleman was holding a home-made contraption.

He assembled the captives and stood them at attention with two confederates by his side. He addressed them all. "Someone in this room is hiding a tracking device within the body. Now I want you all to take a look at this little device, this *bricolage* constructed by yours truly using only materials found at hand. Very clever, I think you will agree. This electromagnet, my friends, it will detect the culprit among you. In this way, we will find out the guilty one. If you have something inside you made of steel, be very much afraid. This device may very well rip it from your body. If you have any clips, pins or plates inside of you, these are made of titanium and you have nothing to fear. I want you to see for yourselves the strength of this magnet. You will notice several ordinary nails that are being held tight to the device. Now you! (addressing the Sergeant-at-Arms), Mr. Marlboro Man, let's see if you are strong enough to pull one even one of those nails away."

"I'll take your word it, Frenchie. Get on with your little show."

The Gentleman Terrorist looked down at his device and smiled. The electromagnet was made of fine, insulated wire wrapped around and around an iron bar. The devise was large and cumbersome, and when plugged in, it drew enough current to dim the lights in the room. The Gentleman was well-pleased.

One at a time, the captives were forced to lie on the concrete floor while one of the assistants passed the magnet, like a wand, up one side of the body and down the other. When passed over the calf of the Navy Pilot, the magnet produced such a sharp pain that he could not prevent himself from crying out. "Aha!" proclaimed the Gentleman in triumph "Why did you not tell us, sir? It would have saved a good deal of trouble." The Navy Pilot remained silent.

The Gentleman went on. "This explains a lot, Mr. Buzz Cut guy – guy who likes to be smug, guy who likes to be stoic, guy who likes to be silent. What do you say for yourself now?" By the end, the Gentleman was screaming. The Navy Pilot remained silent. Two of the terrorists were already flipping him over and tying his hands behind his back. The Navy Pilot was sweating, his jaw was clenching and the veins on his forehead were beginning to stand out. The rest were standing in a circle around him and no one said a word.

"Yes of course, you will say nothing. How about name, rank and serial number? Cute! You are a US Navy Pilot. Of course, we already know all these things. I should have known what you were up to. How could I have been so stupid? You were constantly exercising; performing push-ups and sit-ups all day, walking the perimeter of the room, trying to lead the others in calisthenics. Unsuccessfully, I might add. In this respect, you are not much of a leader. What were you doing? Why, you were recharging the battery in the device that is buried in your leg. The same one we are about to remove and destroy." The Navy Pilots brow was bathed in sweat. Still, he remained silent.

The Gentleman snapped to attention. In his native language, he instructed one of his assistants. "Please put a bullet through his brain. Then we will take him to the other room and extract the device. We will soon see what we are dealing with." Then the Navy Pilot was then shot in front of all. The captives all circled close around him as they came face to face with death for the second time.

The Psychologist screamed into the Gentleman's face "You monster! You horrible man!" In his native language, the Gentleman responded, "Shut her up." And one of the assistants slapped her until she fell down.

The Sergeant-at-Arms cut in, "Now you're picking on a lady. What happened to your French charm?" The same assistant struck him in the face with a rifle butt and bloodied his face.

The two assistants dragged the Navy Pilot's body into another room where they would cut the device out of the back of his calf. After the device was disarmed, the terrorists faced a new challenge. Had the Americans already located them? If so, they had best prepare for an assault.

The stunned captives stared at the blood smear trail that extended all the way across the room and under that same locked door. Near the start of the blood streak was a small divot in the concrete, chipped out by the bullet after it traveled through the Navy Pilot's head. Behind that locked and barred door, the terrorists could be heard. Though they were speaking another language, the captives understood their conspiratorial tone.

The terrorists continued to argue and soon concluded that it was too late to move the hostages. The Americans would be there soon and worst of all would be to be caught in the act of moving. Instead they radioed for reinforcements. Within hours, several dozen more soldiers arrived from the interior of the island. Some of them were no more than children.

The captives found themselves abandoned. No evening meal was served and as it turned out, they would not see their captors again. The sixteen spent a fitful night in hopeful anticipation.

The Raid

The next morning, again there was no breakfast, no terrorists. The captives could hear all kinds of commotion in the locked room behind them. Outside, in the forest around them, they could hear trucks coming and going; gears shifting, honking and yelling.

Among the sixteen, there was some talk of trying to break out, coming mainly from [you guessed it] the Sergeant-at-Arms.

"Bad idea" said the Physiologist. They're all around us. Can't you hear them? They're not concerned about us right now. They have bigger problems. But they're still concerned enough to shoot us. They think a raid is coming to free us and so do I. When it comes, that will be the time to break out." The captives spent the remainder of the day in subdued silence.

At nightfall, SEALs arrived in four helicopters. They arrived at night hoping to gain advantage through the use of night-vison. The first helicopter came from inland and strafed the roof of the building, taking out a sniper. Due to dire time constraints, the SEALs were coming in without a detailed plan of the site. At the first sound of gunfire overhead, The Ski Bum slumped over on the bench where he was sitting and his head landed on the table with a thud. He had been shot between the shoulder blades, and over the next few minutes, died an agonizing death as the others rushed to his side.

A minute later, three more helicopters came in from the direction of the sea and landed a hundred yards in front of the bunker. Soon those inside the bunker could hear gunfire and shouting.

The captives set about making themselves heard and trying to break out. Several shouted in the direction of the front door. Others tried to boost each other up to the second story windows. When that failed, they used the dining table to ram the front door. But the door was heavy and barred from the outside with iron bar. After ramming the door a few times, the table began to fall apart, so they quit.

Meanwhile, the SEALs were engaged in a firefight with guerilla fighters who retreated into the forest. They greatly outnumbered the SEALs, but the SEALs had superior firepower. The retreating fighters holed up behind a wall of sandbags and began to fire at the SEALs. The SEALs soon discovered that forest floor was rigged with trip wires and razor wires, and they advanced slowly. The SEALs were at first reluctant to use their heavier weapons because they did not know where the hostages were and perhaps they were behind that wall of sandbags.

Some of the SEALs stayed behind to attend to the bunker where the hostages were locked inside. One planted plastic explosive on the side of the block wall. He yelled "stay away from this wall" before stepping back to detonate. There was a small explosion, meant to breach the wall of concrete block, but not cause casualties inside. Blocks and pieces of blocks were pulled away and then fifteen captives came crouching out the hole and stepped down onto the dirt roadway.

The SEAL counted and said, "There should be eighteen of you. Where are the other three?"

The Psychologist answered him "We've had three deaths. Two died a while back and their bodies were taken away by our captors. One was hit by a stray bullet just minutes ago and he's still in there."

"Are you sure that individual is dead?"

She was, but the SEAL went in anyway. He lifted the body of the Ski Bum and carried him to the edge of the opening; then placed him on the red-orange volcanic soil beside the wall. As this was happening, the rest of the hostages were escorted under the roaring blades of two helicopters and whisked to safety aboard the Adelaide. After the raid started, the Adelaide had moved to within a couple of miles of shore and on board, the captives who were now no longer captives could hear the battle occurring on the edge of the jungle. The Adelaide would wait there another day for the arrival of the transport ship the USNS Guam and its patrol gunboat, the USS Guam. At that point, the Adelaide would cruise to Darwin RAAF, where the freed hostages would spend several days being checked out medically, before being flown to D.C.

for a hero's welcome.

Back onshore, the SEALs had their firefight under control. Upon learning that all hostages were accounted for, they launched a full-scale attack on the sandbag wall and those behind it. They switched from rifles to grenade launchers and anti-tank missile launchers and soon sent the rag-tag army fleeing for their lives. The SEALs had complete control of that part of the island.

By the noon the next day, the USS Guam made a beach landing. By this time, the services of the troops onboard were barely needed. A clean-up operation was already underway. The SEALs had lined up the bodies of the slain terrorists in the shade beside the bunker. These would eventually become the responsibility of the Indonesian government. There were fifty-seven in total, so the terrorist band had received considerable re-enforcement in the day or so prior to the raid. In addition, many more had escaped into the jungle. Also among the casualties were two SEALs, one dead and one wounded. There was an ice maker on the Adelaide and ice was brought to preserve the bodies, giving preference to the fallen SEAL.

The post-mortem analysis of the scene revealed several interesting facts. First of all, little was left behind in the way of computers or anything else of intelligence value. However, in the area of the smaller rooms, those behind the main hall of the bunker, a closet was opened and a bomb discovered. The bomb was nearly the size of a fifty-five-gallon drum, full of plastic explosive and all kinds of metal designed to serve as shrapnel. It had enough power to reduce the concrete-block bunker to pebbles. It appeared to have a radio-controlled detonator. It also appeared that the terrorists had a back-up plan in case of a raid. If confronted with superior force, they would have hidden in the jungle, while attempting to lure the Americans into the bunker. At that point, it seemed that they were planning to set off the bomb remotely and kill all Americans, both hostages and rescuers. All this speculation led to one obvious question. Why didn't they set off the bomb? They didn't know whether SEALs had entered the bunker. But even so, when facing defeat, why didn't they set off the bomb to kill the hostages and also to see what harm they could due to the rescue operation?

The answer came in a most surprising way. In the Ski Bum's pocket were found two pieces of wire, each several inches long and covered with red plastic insulation. Both wires looked like they had been ripped from places where they had been soldered in place. The USNS Guam had a bomb squad on board and they dismantled the bomb. The Ski Bum's body was aboard the Adelaide. Once the bomb was cleared by the bomb squad, the two wires were taken back to the bunker and sure enough, the fractured solder on them matched exactly to places on the bomb. That's all the forensics that were needed. The Ski Bum had successfully disarmed the bomb, preventing the death of all the other hostages. Speculation began about how the Ski Bum had gotten access to the closet and the bomb. All the surviving hostages agreed to be discrete; in other words, to say they didn't know. Mrs. White required some convincing.

Postscript

Cut to almost a week later and a press conference at the White house. President McKelly began "Good afternoon, my fellow Americans. Today is a bittersweet occasion as we honor the success of Operation Haystack and of Operation Lily Pad. Eight days ago, these missions culminated in the liberation of fifteen American hostages who were held on the island of East Timor for seven days.

"As you all know, on the night of January the twenty-seventh, terrorists staged an attack on the Mount Lasser Ski Resort in California. The terrorists set off an avalanche that buried one

hundred and ninety. Of those, only seven have survived. After the avalanche had passed, the terrorists flew by helicopter from their position high on Mount Lasser to the top of The Tubes night club. Once inside, they took nineteen hostages and killed one American before taking the hostages, also by helicopter, to a staging site in the Mendocino National Forest. From there, they took the hostages by jet to the remote island of East Timor. The map behind me shows the location of that island in the far eastern part of Indonesia and adjacent to Australia.

"Soon after American intelligence located the hostages in East Timor, Navy SEAL Team 6 launched the raid that freed those hostages. The raid was launched from Darwin Royal Australian Air Force Base. On behalf of the American people, I would like to express our thanks to Australian government and to members of the Australian military for their crucial role in the success of this mission.

"At the panel behind me are the sixteen surviving hostages. They are, from your left to your right, Arnold Powers, Dolores Del Rio, Martin Pelli, Evet St. Rob, Ian Underwood, Claudia Talmadge, Victor Forzley, Marcus McCabe, Carol Osterberg, Elytra Noll, Lauren Campbell, Petra Martens, Ryan Sinclair, Hi Makanudo, Martha "Sunny" Fine, and Janet White. At this time, I would also like to acknowledge the three American hostages who are not with us today. Kenneth Holliman died of natural causes. Colonel Richard Neudeck was a retired Navy Pilot. While still in the military, he had a tracking device implanted in his leg. This device allowed us to locate the terrorists. Unfortunately, he was killed by the terrorists once they found out he had the device. Fulton Hale disarmed a bomb in the bunker where the hostages were kept and probably saved the lives of all. In a separate ceremony, Colonel Neudeck and Mr. Hale will receive the Secretary of Defense Medal for Valor posthumously.

"A total of one hundred and eighty-eight Americans lost their lives as a direct result of this tragedy and the list of their names is too long for me to read to you today. However, their names will soon be made public and plans are underway to construct a memorial in their honor."

The President introduced the surviving members of US Navy Seal Team Six and then he invited members of the press to address their questions to those on the stage. For the next hour, the SEALs and the hostages told their stories.

One question, near the end: "We heard that there may be an upcoming marriage between two of the surviving hostages, any truth to that?" To great applause, Hi and Sunny announced their plans to be married at Mount Lasser in the Spring. "Where will you honeymoon?" Sunny answered "We don't know yet, but if you suggest East Timor, I will literally kill you."